THE MERMAID'S TALE

(人魚紀)

THE MERMAID'S TALE

(人魚紀)

LEE WEI-JING

(李維菁)

English translation by
Darryl Sterk

SCRIBNER

LONDON NEW YORK SYDNEY TORONTO NEW DELHI

First published in Great Britain by Scribner,
an imprint of Simon & Schuster UK Ltd, 2022

Originally published in Taiwan by ThinKingdom Media Group Ltd.
English Translation Copyright © 2022 ThinKingdom Media Group Ltd. c/o The
Grayhawk Agency in association with Georgina Capel Associates Ltd.

1 3 5 7 9 10 8 6 4 2

Simon & Schuster UK Ltd
1st Floor
222 Gray's Inn Road
London WC1X 8HB

www.simonandschuster.co.uk
www.simonandschuster.com.au
www.simonandschuster.co.in

Simon & Schuster Australia, Sydney
Simon & Schuster India, New Delhi

A CIP catalogue record for this book
is available from the British Library

Trade Paperback ISBN: 978-1-3985-0760-9
eBook ISBN: 978-1-3985-0761-6

Typeset in Palatino by M Rules
Printed and bound by CPI Group (UK) Ltd, Croydon CR0 4YY

Contents

Translator's Note

Lee Wei-Jing emailed me in late 2016 to ask if I had time to translate two chapters from her novel *La Dolce Vita*. I made the time, and delivered the translations to her in early 2017. The next news I had of her was her tragic death from cancer in November 2018. She'd just finished a novel entitled *The Mermaid's Tale*, which would be published in 2019 and honoured with a national literary award in December of the same year. At the invitation of Gray Tan, who has been handling the foreign rights of Lee's fiction, I prepared a draft translation in January 2020. I'd like to thank Gray and all the others who have helped me during the revision process.

A number of fellow translators and editors helped me put the right words in the right order. Translator Scott Faul came up with 'cotton candy clouds', which copy editor Charlotte Chapman changed to 'candyfloss clouds' to match British usage. Copy editor Tamsin Shelton suggested 'you can't judge a dancer by the dress'. Translator Canaan Morse, who edited an earlier version of the first three chapters of the translation for *Books From Taiwan*, recommended 'the tumbling procession of the everyday'. Translator Anna Holmwood inspired Summer's 'virtual fist pump'. Editor Jeff Lindstrom proposed that I call Summer 'a contender'. Thanks to my wife, Joey Su, Summer has a 'pancake butt'. Finally, Erin Bomboy, the author of *The Winner*, is the source of 'drilling the syllabus' and 'fulfilling the promise of the knee', both in her splendidly written ballroom dance novel and in her helpful reply to my email about *The Mermaid's Tale*.

Unlike me, Erin Bomboy has been a professional dancer and dance critic, someone who knows what she's talking about when it comes to ballroom dance. If I have managed to make the dance descriptions in *The Mermaid's Tale* plausible, it's partly thanks to her. I'm also grateful to Claire Yen, Anna Lee and Shih-Ting Liang, who replied to my public request for assistance with Chinese dance terminology, and for their technical explanations and demonstrations I'd like to thank my brother Lindsay Sterk and my friend Terrence Russell. Terry gave me a lot of guidance just by sending me the photo of Iveta Lukosiute and Gherman Mustuc featured on the opposite page, which I spent a lot of time poring over when I was translating chapter 7.

I'm also thankful to Jessie Hsieh and to Professor Diana

Gherman Mustuc and Iveta Lukosiute dancing a
Classical Showdance number called 'La Jazz Hot'.

Yun-Hsien Lin, Lee Wei-Jing's sister-in-law, for checking
the translation for accuracy.

Diana helped me get to know the late author in ways
that greatly enriched my understanding of the novel. For
instance, Summer's best friend, whom I had been calling Sunny, was probably named after Kimura Mitsuki,
the daughter of one of Lee Wei-Jing's favourite sing-
ers. Another favourite singer of hers was Cher, whose

flamboyant style Mitsuki channels in the dance competition at the end of chapter 5. Margaret Atwood was one of Lee Wei-Jing's favourite writers, *The Handmaid's Tale* one of her favourite novels, which she may have revisited by watching the Hulu adaptation. With a suggestive pun on tail, *The Mermaid's Tale* can be read as a literary homage. Diana also informed me that Lee Wei-Jing's academic background was in agronomy, not in English literature, as I had assumed. An agronomist could understand the metaphor of the mermaid in the light of evolution. Summer is a mermaid who left the ocean to evolve into a human in an urban habitat, while the grass she cultivated in her underwater garden is an angiosperm, a flowering plant whose ancestors left the land to recolonize the ocean. As Paul Simon puts it, 'We are born and born again, like the waves of the sea.'

Lee Wei-Jing's mermaid is at home in the sea, a metaphor for the realm of freedom one enters when one steps on the dance floor. The association of water and dancing is more than implicit in the Chinese vocabulary of dance, for instance the fact that a dance floor is literally a 'dance pool' (*wuchi* 舞池). What does water have to do with freedom? It's the closest most of us get to weightlessness; in water, buoyancy frees us from the pull of gravity, which brings us all crashing down sooner or later on land. It is in this context that we can understand Lee Wei-Jing's repeated references to *jianghu* (江湖, literally 'rivers' and 'lakes').* *Jianghu* is a literary genre and imaginary realm populated by mostly righteous outlaws, drifters who are free to break imperial law, if not the law of *jianghu*. Like Summer as a would-be ballroom dancer, they, too, have to follow the rules.

As Summer explains in chapter 2, ballroom dancers have to follow the rule of men lead, women follow, but in Latin dances like the rumba, the leader can let the follower go. As a result, '[f]or at least part of every dance, the girl can dance her own steps, choose her own line – she's free.' I took this sentiment to heart in my approach to the translation. I added chapter headings and assigned mythopoeic material to a prelude and an interlude. Usually, I would consult with the author about such modifications, but in this case that wasn't possible. I'm grateful to Lee Wei-Jing's family for approving the way I have swum through the sea of her words.

---

* Notice that chí 池, jiāng 江 and hú 湖 share the water radical (氵).

Prelude

STRANDED

Every morning, right before sunrise, I feel like stepping into the blue and swimming off until I vanish at the margin of sea and sky.

But I just keep standing here, every time. I never go in. Sometimes it feels like I've been standing here for ever.

Look, my heels have sunk deep into the fine white sand, as if I am rooted in the beach, as if I've transplanted myself to the shore.

Look, I've turned bright red, as if badly burned from so much sun. But actually it's a rash, not a burn. My sun allergy has been acting up again, causing me to break out in hives, from head to toe. I have them on my scalp, my forehead, my cheeks, my neck, my armpits, my private parts, my bum crack, the insides of my thighs, and even the soles of my feet. My skin looks like candyfloss clouds at dawn, though

1

it won't look like that for much longer if I keep scratching these hives until they bleed.

I've had this allergy before, but never this badly. I've had hives before, but never this itchy. I feel a bit feverish.

1

Nasty Creatures

One day about a decade ago, when I was already well on the wrong side of thirty but still in the habit of calling myself 'young', my landlord arrived unannounced to collect the rent, first thing in the morning. I was still lying in bed. I was awake, but I really didn't want to get up. The sound of the buzzer was so harsh, and he was jabbing at it with such urgency, that it was like a howling ghost had come to haunt me. For what? I'd never done anything in my entire rotten life to anyone, let alone him, to deserve this. But he kept buzzing that buzzer, over and over, like a prosecutor pounding the table.

I could sense his obstinacy, his righteous indignation, his rising rage.

He wasn't going to let up, so I gave in. I dragged myself out of bed, found one slipper and tried in vain to find its mate. I had to hop out across the balcony.

My landlord started yelling as soon as I opened the door. 'What the hell were you doing in there, you nasty creature? Do you know how long I've been standing here? Didn't want to see me, eh? It's that time of the month again, and you know what I mean. If you can't pay the rent, you should tell me *before* I come to collect. I can give you a few days' grace period, no problem. It's fine. *Justdon'tkeepmewaitinglikethat!'*

All my irritation, which had been swelling ever since I was woken in the middle of the night, subsided in an instant at the sight of him. I started to tremble. My mouth went dry.

Somehow, he'd managed to stick half a dozen hair clips into his sparse, closely cropped white hair. He was wearing clip-on earrings with purple pearl pendants, three necklaces of pastel shells – purple, silver and gold – and as many rings as he could fit on his fingers. He'd forced mauve-tinted lenses into his fuddy-duddy frames. Otherwise he was your typical Taiwanese retiree, an old fart in a grubby singlet, which he'd matched with shapeless shorts and cracked flip-flops.

I tried not to let my surprise show. I didn't want to hurt his feelings.

I wanted to tell him I had the money, I just didn't want to have to get up so early.

'Please don't come first thing in the morning without letting me know in advance!' I wanted to say. 'I go to bed

4

late. If you really have to come without telling me before-hand, please wait until the afternoon.'

But I didn't say anything. I guessed it would have been no use. The old fellow was so obviously deranged that I doubted anything I could have said would have got through to him.

It would be better to just let him vent.

'I've got the money in my account,' I whispered, finally. 'I just have to withdraw it. Would you mind if I dropped it off downstairs this afternoon?'

'Well, you could have told me yesterday!' The purple pendants were swaying slightly. The veins at his temples were pulsating. 'Didn't I say I'd give you a few days' grace if you'd just let me know?'

Without waiting for my reply, he turned and teetered slowly down the stairs. He stopped at the turn and pressed his palms to his cheeks, like he was shocked, or like he had an itch to scratch. Could he be having a heart attack? Or did he think he was Beyoncé? Apparently, he did. He tossed his head, spilling thick tresses he didn't have over his shoulder, and ran his palms down his sides to his waist. Elbows out, he smiled a shy, yet somehow coy, even sassy, smile. He flirted with some invisible presence that was hanging in mid-air, then took that smile with him down the remaining stairs.

I closed the door, hopped back across the balcony and

flopped on to the sofa I'd put right outside the sliding door. I chuckled, but then I started shuddering, and I couldn't stop.

An old man on my doorstep wearing cheap jewellery had freaked me out. I don't know why I got so upset, but I did. I felt as if I'd been in the presence of a psychopath, or a malevolent supernatural power.

Whatever he was acting out must have been building in him for quite some time, because, now I thought about it, there had already been a sign.

The previous month he'd come to collect the rent wearing another necklace, of purple puka shells. Assuming a grandchild had gone on a Polynesian cruise and bought it for Grandpa at the souvenir shop, I didn't think much of it at the time, but now that he'd shown up in all those other accessories, flicking non-existent hair like he was trying to make himself look fetching, it took on a new significance.

Something had come undone in him, like a split end or a loose thread. Perhaps it was just a thread that had come loose in life, a thread that the trundling Wheel of Time would roll into the tumbling procession of the everyday. It was deviant, but deviations are temporary. It couldn't be considered a part of the regular rhythm of life, and wasn't so destructive it could blow up the logic of everyday normality. So what if it was deviant?

It was abnormal, no question about it; but anything abnormal is temporary by definition. It wouldn't alter the regular rhythm of life. It wouldn't explode the logic of my mundane existence. So what if it was abnormal? It didn't matter.

I lay there trying to reassure myself until I shuddered again, with cold this time. It can get quite chilly in the morning in the middle of a Taipei winter. Too lethargic to go in and get a quilt, I curled up on the sofa like a shrimp.

I wasn't tired, just sluggish, and I couldn't shake the feeling off.

I'd been woken up at about four in the morning when a woman somewhere nearby cried out, as if in pain. Her cries got louder and louder, clearer and clearer, so loud and clear that at times it sounded as if she were crying right outside my flat.

I got up, slid the door open and looked out into the night, to see if I could follow the sound to its source, out of curiosity and in case I needed to call the police. I thought I'd better keep the light off. But by this point the lights had started to come on in other people's flats. Soon there were bare-chested men in boxer shorts standing on balconies trying, like me, to figure out where the woman was. It sounded like she was up on the seventh or eighth floor of one of the nearby mid-rises.

She would scream from time to time, as though being hit. The rest of the time she tried to stifle her sobs, like she was cowering in the corner, trying not to provoke her abuser. The men on balconies had been joined by anxious wives at windows. 'Is she in the west block?' one man asked his neighbour. 'Should we call 119?'

But then the woman's cry changed into a breathy, flirtatious sigh, almost like a moan of pleasure. The men and women standing vigilant on balconies or by windows were gobsmacked. *Was that what I think it was?*

There it was again, and this time anyone with ears could tell she was moaning.

Lights that had been flipped on were flipped off again, as what had seemed to be a suspense thriller had turned into an absurd farce. 'All right, you two, give it a rest!' one man hollered sternly into the darkness. 'You've woken up enough people for one night.'

I thought it was hilarious. I had to keep myself from laughing out loud. It was the most dramatic night I'd had in a long time.

I went back to bed but I just couldn't get over it, so I felt my way back to the door.

By then everyone had turned off the lights and gone to sleep. I felt a bit lonely.

I should try to get back to sleep, I thought. Sleep would give me energy to dance. I had a lesson tomorrow. Today, actually.

For the longest time, the only thing that had injected any drama into my humdrum days was ballroom dancing.

2

THE TWO BIGGEST FEARS OF ANY BEGINNING BALLROOM DANCER

The biggest fear for people who take up ballroom dancing is not finding a partner. A lot of beginners dance for quite a while without finding Mr or Ms Right. The only chance they get to pair up with someone is when they dance with their teacher in a one-on-one lesson, or with a random stranger in a group class, perhaps someone whose partner is absent that day. But that's a poor substitute for a partner, someone who belongs to you and you alone.

I hadn't met Mr Right, but with a bit of luck, I thought, I'd find him. I was spending quite a bit of time, energy and money learning how to dance. It was my only significant expense. I was taking an individual lesson and a group class, both with the same teacher. With Donny's help, I

hoped to get really good – at least good enough that someone decent would want to dance with me.

I took my individual lesson at the Fortress, the biggest
dance studio in Taiwan. While the advanced students and
competitors marked their routines, I practised the basics
under Donny's exacting eye. Just getting the basic steps
right took a great deal of time. Actually, according to
Donny, you practised these steps for life.

The group class was held at an activity centre. The students were mostly older, actually quite a bit older, than
me. It was known as the 'aunties and uncles' class. Those
aunties and uncles were really good. Donny taught them
the flowery moves debuted by the top pros in international
competition. Learning moves like that made the aunties
feel they were getting their money's worth.

The two classes were complementary. I could pick
up new moves in group class and hone my technique
in the individual lessons. Then it was up to me to practise at home.

Donny said he'd keep an eye out at the Fortress in case
anyone needed a partner. He didn't need to tell me that
the chances were slim. Those studio dancers all had their
hearts set on competition, and I had taken ballroom up
too late to be competitive. I was more likely to find a partner in the aunties and uncles class, particularly because
it wasn't just an aunties and uncles class any more. On

the strength of Donny's reputation, younger dancers had started coming, too. Maybe someone unattached would show up.

'Don't worry,' Donny would say. 'You just keep practising, see where you get.' I was always reminded of what he'd left unsaid.

I'd seen enough cases where single dancers never found a partner. In every case, they quit sooner or later. If you can't find a partner, it's hard to practise. It isn't just that it's difficult to learn the movements without a partner. Imagine yourself dancing alone while pairs of dancers swirl around you. They're all too busy getting the steps right and maintaining a connection to notice anyone who's left out. To anyone who *has* ended up alone, it doesn't seem that way. You'd feel excluded, right? Anyone would. No matter how determined they are, new dancers who can't find partners tend to get discouraged after a week or two. After a month or two they can't take it any more. Then they just stop coming.

I once watched an interview with a celebrity dance teacher who claimed that finding a dance partner is the same as finding a life partner. Things will just click if the right person appears. The thing is to make sure you're ready when the time comes.

To a lot of my classmates, it was the gospel truth. To them, finding a dance partner really was like love at first sight, the logic of romance – to the extent that romance has any logic. As long as you're ready, they said, as long as you wait long enough, you'll find him, or he'll find you.

Yes and no. I'm sure there is some truth to the comparison between finding your dance partner and meeting your soulmate. But in the real world, the right person doesn't have to appear, because you can choose to stay single, you can decide not to get hitched, especially these days. In the world of ballroom dancing, by contrast, you need a partner. If you haven't paired up with someone, you can't get in the front door, let alone on to the dance floor. You'll never get admitted into that world, no matter who initiates you, no matter who your teacher is.

But at that time I wanted to believe that as long as I trained hard enough, I would meet my match sooner or later, and we would get better together, like competitors. We couldn't go pro but we could at least compete as amateurs. Donny would be happy for me, for sure.

I had to be realistic, no matter what, I told myself. At the time, being realistic meant that I had to keep training on my own. I couldn't just wait for Mr Right to waltz into my life before I made the first move.

At the height of my training, I was taking eight hours of dance classes over four days a week. The two most intense hours of my week were on the two days I went to the Fortress, for an hour each time. The studio classroom was full of young competitors, their high spirits and their pheromones. They always seemed poised and ready, and bursting with energy. When I walked in they might be stretching at the barres or practising specific steps. Regardless, every one of them was focused on his or her body – on the body that was reflected in the full-length wraparound mirrors.

'The mirror is a dancer's best friend,' Donny said. 'The mirror will tell you where your problems are, if you have eyes to see. Most people don't. Mostly people can't see where they've gone wrong even when it's right there in front of them. If they can't see, there's no hope for them. If they can, then they've got the chance to get really good. Or they go nuts.'

On the other two days, I had the aunties and uncles class at the activity centre, for three hours each time. In a typical group class, most people, no matter how much they enjoy it, are only doing it for fun. For students like that, a lot depends on how good the teacher is. Donny was good, both as a dancer and a teacher. His sincere dedication warmed the hearts of those older students, no matter how long they'd been dancing, and some of them had been at it for a long, long time. Some of them were teachers in their own right, but obviously they felt they had room for improvement, and something to learn from Donny.

Indeed, Donny wasn't just dedicated, he was demanding. Nobody dared to cut corners in his class. Everyone's will to better him- or herself had been summoned up by this bright young man. Now the aunties and uncles were just as devoted to the art of dance as their juniors at the studio. But the smell – well, it was a different story.

Four days each week, I'd get home having sweated so much that my underwear would still be damp.

On the other three days, I'd train at home, practising the basic steps, drilling the syllabus or miming along to videos on YouTube. I also had to work my core, to give myself the kind of body I needed for dancing. 'Because,' Donny said, 'a body without a core is like a tree without a trunk.'

I'd started too late to have any hope of being an advanced competitor, but I still wanted to get a bit closer to perfect dancing form. I thought I had it in me to be a true dancer, at least. I would have been embarrassed to tell anyone, but I wanted to dance with a formal perfection that the cognoscenti could not help but admire, and not like someone who'd taken up social dance as a pastime. If I just wanted a way to pass the time, I could square dance with the seniors at the local park on a Sunday morning.

I'd work on whatever Donny taught, wherever he thought I fell short. He was my favourite person in the world. I looked up to him and counted on him. I was lost at sea in the world of partner dance, and Donny was a piece of driftwood I was clinging to, the only thing that was keeping me afloat.

Whatever folks say about love, I hadn't chosen Donny blindly. I knew what I was looking for in a teacher, or at least the kind of teacher I wanted to avoid, by the time he floated by. I had taken some classes and lessons with a few other teachers, but like a lot of people who give dance a try, I always ended up feeling disappointed, even cheated.

I'd studied with a few professionals who were still competing, and with a few former competitors who were teaching to pay the bills. None of them took teaching seriously, at least not when they were teaching me. They never got me to practise the basics. They would demonstrate a few steps, put the music on and dance me in circles until the time was up.

That's what partner dancing is like if it's just a social activity. All the woman has to do is relax and let the man lead, and she can while the evening away, happy as a princess. That's all those teachers do – turn you in circles, sending the hem of your dress flying. They make you feel like you can actually dance, but then time's up, class dismissed. You've danced for an hour and ended up with nothing but well-stroked vanity. For some ladies, dance lessons are a substitute for romance. Some of them end a lesson all hot and bothered, flushed with fantasy. As with all such arrangements, the teacher only plays along for the time the student has paid for. If the student sticks around afterwards, the teacher will ignore her and chat with his fellow competitors.

If the teacher comes from a competitive background, he'll care more about dance than making money, believe it or not. He'll care about dancers as long as they are his fellow competitors – his brothers or sisters in arms. When a teacher like that takes students, he'll ask: did you take dance in school, do you have a degree in physical education, have you studied at all? If your answer is yes to any of these questions, and you appear to have ambition and talent, and might even have what it takes to compete, then he'll address you as a fellow artist and hold you to the highest standard. If, on the other hand, your answers are all no, and you're already on the wrong side of twenty, he'll conclude that no amount of training is going to turn you into a competitor; you're never going to make it. Then he'll start wondering: can you help support me financially? Do you, in other words, have what it takes to be a cash machine? And if you are a rich older lady, you might be in want of one of those slick-haired, sweet-mouthed mercenaries who half-arses his way across the dance floor, a bandit in the world of ballroom dance. He'll ask himself if you have what it takes to be a bank vault. He'll sweet-talk you out of everything, if you're not careful.

I was lucky enough to avoid getting stuck with this kind of teacher, because I was never going to go pro and obviously I wasn't rich, or a cougar. Whether competitor or crook, the teacher soon realised I didn't have what it took to be whatever he wanted me to be. In his eyes, I was never going to amount to anything. I'd soon realise I'd been made a fool of. Teachers like that were contemptuous of or simply indifferent to earnest outsiders looking longingly in, which is to say students like me. They made me feel disrespected, like a second-class citizen in the country of dance.

So I was getting discouraged by the time I first heard about Donny from a girlfriend who was nicknamed after the heroine of *Princess Mononoke* and who claimed to be just as interested in learning how to dance as I was. Princess had already been to observe the aunties and uncles class, and asked me to come and check it out. An aunties and uncles class? That was the first I'd heard of such a thing. I pictured a couple of dozen old ladies and gentlemen doing social dance, or worse. There was no way the teacher could be any good. I was sure the teacher of a class like that must be pretending to be something he wasn't. I said I wasn't interested in taking a class with another poser.

'Come on, give him a chance,' she told me. 'At least come and have a look.' If I did, she said, I'd understand why she'd recommended him.

A couple of months passed and I still hadn't found a teacher. So I finally went to that group class.

I was blown away the moment I walked in and saw several dozen pairs of stylish, self-confident dancers strutting their stuff around the room. I didn't initially notice the dancers were old enough to be my aunties and uncles. I just felt a kind of intense dedication. It was a physical confidence, an energy that raced through the room, like a wildfire. Then I saw the teacher. Just standing there clapping, marking time, Donny was the real deal: he had a powerful presence, a kind of earnest intensity that you noticed as soon as you entered the room. With the force and warmth of the morning sun, he barked at the aunties and uncles like they were contenders. 'Dance the details!' he said, as if at that moment there wasn't anything more important than getting the finer points of some transition right. Donny's passion for the art of dance was infectious; it fairly gushed out of him, flooding the room with charged particles. The place was humming.

Then he demonstrated a sequence. With all the rapid flexions and extensions of his muscles, he translated the music, bar by bar, into movement, with a smile playing at the edge of his lips. Throughout, he kept his axis straight and his centre of gravity low. The foundation of his often extravagant flourishes was stability.

At the end of the demonstration, he spun around and

stopped. I finally saw him from the front. Small eyes, pale skin, square jaw, a body toned by training, with prominent bones. He wasn't exactly good-looking, but when he started dancing he was a superstar.

This is a dancer! I thought, amazed at how he moved his body. I was also impressed by the way he treated his students. He was unfailingly polite, and he took every question seriously. He obviously wanted to share his art with anyone who wanted to understand, to the extent they *could* understand. He was, I thought, a living Confucius of the cha-cha, a pedagogue who must aspire to the ideal of 'education without discrimination'. He must be an Apostle Thomas of the jive. Yes, I was convinced he had a calling – to spread the gospel of Latin dance.

Watching Donny demonstrate, I heard a wordless call. And what did I call out in reply? This is my teacher!

'Let's start next week,' I said to Princess, during the break. She was delighted.

Before that day I'd had no respect for older amateur dancers like the aunties and uncles, but now I knew there were crouching tigers and hidden dragons in the world of ballroom dance – like the master martial artists who prefer seclusion to society, privacy to fame, in those old Chinese novels about *jianghu*, a realm of mostly righteous outlaws.

So what was the difference between aunties and uncles on the one hand and the studio competitors on the other, besides the smell? It was in the fundamentals. The aunties and uncles had not spent enough time on the basics, repeating the simplest steps ad infinitum until they were second nature. They hadn't run enough rounds around the room or drilled the syllabus enough. That kind of training is tedious, unrewarding. It doesn't give you any immediate sense of achievement. And, they thought, they already knew the basic footwork, so why practise it over and over, every day? They wanted Donny to teach them the latest, the most difficult and intricate steps, the ones the world champions were dancing. But unlike the world champions, the aunties and uncles hadn't spent anywhere near enough time laying the foundation. It's like playing the piano. Scales are the most monotonous, and the most unglamorous, part of practice, but the most virtuosic concert pianist still does them religiously. Everyone wants to learn new pieces, but if you don't keep doing your scales it's no use. You can learn all the pieces you want, but you'll never get anywhere; nobody will ever pay to hear you play.

The other thing the aunties and uncles had neglected was sit-ups and squats. Much more than a concert pianist, a dancer has got to develop core stability, which the aunties and uncles just didn't have. They didn't maintain a steady axis; they wobbled. They didn't stay erect; they slouched.

20

And as they didn't tuck in their tailbones, they couldn't funnel force through their pelvises. Donny might be fifteen kilos lighter, but he seemed more solid than any of them.

That said, they were still amazing, dancing at that level at that age – two or even three decades older than me, some of them. There were sixty-year-olds in that class who had started in middle age and were now much more advanced than me. Hearing their stories helped me find my fighting spirit.

I took the group class for two months before I asked Donny if he had time for an individual lesson. I wanted to see how the pros in the studio trained.

I told him I wanted to lay the foundation, to dance the details – no, the details of the details. I wanted to let him know I understood.

'Teach me like you would a competitor,' I said, blushing.

Donny was non-committal. He looked at me sceptically. I realised that he had another side. He was always bright and forthright in class, but he could obviously be a bit of a bitch when he wanted to. He wasn't above posturing.

He could put on all the airs he wanted – I didn't care. Sensing that I wasn't going to give up without a fight, he told me to come and give it a try. 'We'll see,' he said. When he said the same thing after the first lesson, I was just as determined to take the second and the third. I wanted to prove myself to him. I wanted to show him how serious I was. If he really had the missionary zeal I had intuited in him the first time I watched him dance, he would take me as his disciple, because my intense earnestness would touch him, too.

In the second and third lessons Donny kept hinting that he wished I'd stop coming, or that I'd find another teacher. I noticed the hints at the time, but only grasped what he was hinting at in retrospect. I just kept going, full speed ahead. I kept getting him to give little old me expensive individual instruction.

I forget how many times it took before Donny finally accepted me, as a student and as a friend. Maybe he finally realised what a warm-hearted, guileless person I was.

When I got on Donny's good side, he revealed that he'd had no intention of teaching me on a long-term basis, not just because I was too old but also because I seemed odd. He wasn't sure what to make of me. Was I a wimp? It certainly seemed that way, but then I'd get really intense on him, either staring or refusing to make eye contact. And though I was long-limbed, I wasn't graceful when I swung round. I was gawky.

I just didn't seem to look the part, Donny said. But you can't judge a dancer by their dress.

As Donny soon discovered, I had an amazing natural feeling for dance. I was really observant; I had a keen eye and a keen ear. I was also dedicated. I'd keep practising at home until I got the steps down pat. I improved by leaps and bounds. Now it was Donny's turn to be impressed.

'If you'd started when you were younger, you'd be an amazing dancer by now.'

'How can you tell?'

'You've just got the qualities of a good woman dancer.'

'What qualities are those?'

'Hungry, intuitive, ill-tempered, bloody minded.'

Before dance became a part of my life, I had kept things simple. I didn't have a regular job, but what did I need one for? If your only expenses are food and rent, you really don't need that much to get by.

I imagined myself as a bubble drifting along in my own tiny corner of a vast ocean. Big fish swam past and I'd hide in the coral. Little fish swam by and I'd follow along in their wake. So what if I was small? I was like an eye, and I got to see the sights: here a glimmer, there a sparkle, over there a gleam. Sometimes I was tempted to float up to the surface and refract the sunlight into a faint rainbow for an instant that would seem like an eternity. Then I would burst. It wouldn't be a bad way to go.

But when dance entered my life, especially after Donny came on the scene, everything changed. I became doggedly determined. I had desire and ambition. I wore soft, flat-soled shoes when I started; eventually I could wear 2½-inch heels. The steps that went too fast at first, eventually I could follow.

More importantly, I started to refine the way I moved; soon my limbs were like seagrass swaying with the swells. I sensed the unity of body with rhythm and melody; I felt an instinctive joy.

At some point I became obsessed with the idea that I had the right to control my body. Soon I gained more of an ability to get it to do what I wanted. I wasn't so helpless after all.

I also learned how to be with a partner. Though I hadn't been touched in years, I was still capable of intimate physical response, and of rapture. I could soar along, as if uplifted by a warm, tender wave. With a partner, you can assume amazing forms and express yourself in unexpected ways. There are so many things you could do with a partner that you can't do alone. But there is a catch.

'Men lead, women follow? Sounds like a chauvinist dance to me,' I complained.

'Yeah, but those are the rules,' Donny said. 'I have to follow them, too.'

Competitive ballroom is divided into two categories, Standard and Latin. There are five dances in each category. The Standard dances are the waltz, the tango, the foxtrot, the Viennese waltz and the quickstep; the Latin dances are the rumba, the cha-cha, the samba, the jive and the paso doble. The woman's skirt is below the knee in Standard dances, above in Latin. Standard dances are slow and elegant; Latin dances are fiery and bold.

I only learned the five Latin dances. I didn't like Standard.

Donny didn't, either. 'When you waltz, you have to keep pressing your lower body against the girl. I. Don't. Want. To.'

So what are the individual Latin dances like? The rumba is sultry. It's the dance of lovers who cannot tear themselves away from each other. The cha-cha is all about pursuit and flirtation. The samba is like the carnival in Rio, a colourful celebration. And the jive? Just think of it as more than friends but less than lovers. It's happy and playful.

'What about the paso doble?' I asked. The paso doble is the bullfight dance. Of all the dances, it's the most straightforward, with only two pieces of music to dance to. For the woman, it's also the most humiliating and exasperating. The man is the matador. There are two roles for the woman to play. She might be the matador's fluttering red cape or she might be the bull.

The interaction between the partners seemed so different in the paso doble, if not entirely lacking. There was no back and forth, no push and pull, or not that I could feel. There was no sense of a magnetic field attracting the partners or pushing them apart. There was only the bullfighter and the bull. And the outcome was always the same: the bull had to die.

'Why?'

'There's no why; those are the rules.'

That's the way it was. Those were the rules, and they couldn't be changed. If I wanted to do Latin dance, I had to follow the rules.

Rule number one was that it was a partner dance.

Rule number two was that men lead, women follow.

At least in Latin dancing you can bend the second rule, just a little, because the leader can let his partner go, momentarily losing control of her. For at least part of every dance, the girl can dance her own steps, choose her own line – she's free. But Latin was the same as Standard with respect to partnership. A single person can't do it; no odd numbers are allowed.

If the biggest fear for a ballroom dance beginner is not finding a partner, then the second biggest fear, as I realised shortly after joining the group class with Donny, is getting stuck with a partner who isn't any good. You wouldn't want to dance too many times with a partner like that, or else they might assume, or your classmates and teacher might start to assume, that you were a pair.

The person I was in danger of getting stuck with was

actually my girlfriend Princess. Even I could tell that she just wasn't any good. Now that Donny had whetted my appetite in individual class, I had some idea of what the interaction between the partners was supposed to be. I had a sense of precision and economy. I found her amateurish-ness, her lack of co-ordination or attention to form harder and harder to stand. Dancing with her was just holding hands and fumbling around. After class I felt like I'd been bumped and scratched all over.

She was happy no matter what. She was always bubbly and vivacious. Surrounded by ladies twice her age, she was self-possessed. But she had no reason to be. She had a bad sense of rhythm, and was always a beat behind. And she could never remember the steps. If you just remember the gist, you can't dance the details; you dance however you want, and when you make a mistake you laugh it off. If your partner gets upset, well then blame it on her.

'What went wrong just now?' I asked once, faking a smile. We'd got out of sync for the umpteenth time.

I was hoping she'd reflect on her shortcomings, or at least apologise. But she didn't.

'Hey,' she said to the auntie who happened to be closest to us at that moment. 'Summer says she can't dance that thing we were just doing. Can you show her?'

Well, obviously you're the problem, I thought. I was so angry I couldn't speak. If she didn't know her rhythm was off, if she couldn't see she'd failed to follow the sequence, then she was doomed. It didn't matter how hard she tried. No – the problem was that it didn't matter to her. For her, dancing was just a chance to show how pretty she was.

Why did she even want to take a dance class in the first place? Unlike me, she had an active social life. She'd go out to a movie with her friends and come late. I'd be fuming by the time she arrived, and it never got any better.

The worst part was that Princess had volunteered to lead. She said she would let me dance the girl's part, out of friendship. I was embarrassed, because she was a lot more feminine than me. And I felt dubious, because she liked flaunting her appearance so much. Why would she want to dance the guy's part when it would afford her few opportunities to do so? If a ballroom couple can be likened to a bouquet in a florist's window, the girl would be the flower, while the man would be the wrapper. Why would Princess want to be the wrapper?

Whatever her motive was, she just couldn't do it. She was a leader who didn't lead. Dancing with her, I'd got into the bad habit of stepping just ahead of the beat, to try to push or pull us back into tempo, as if too fast and too slow would cancel each other out, as if two wrongs could make a right. In doing so, I was trying to take over the leader's task. I knew that the longer this went on the worse I would dance. My bad habit would ruin everything. If you're ambitious about dance, if you ever want to compete, you have to follow the rules. There's no future for a girl who leads. I wanted out.

I felt guilty. Princess was the one who'd discovered Donny and taken me to see him in the first place. I wouldn't be there if it weren't for her.

But at this rate, I would never improve. She was holding me back. I wanted to break up with her.

Donny told me to calm down. He agreed about the need for a split, but said I needed to wait. I would know when it was time.

I was about to solve one problem, only to create another. If I ditched Princess, who would dance with her? And who would dance with me?

I tried to think positively. At least by that point I had a good idea of what I was looking for in a partner.

There was a young engaged couple in the group class who had joined not long before Princess took me and who were about the same age as me. Like me, they were also taking an individual lesson, actually a two-on-one lesson, with Donny. The man was big and strong, but had a baby face. The girl was petite, but her face was just as round. We called them Big Round and Little Round. Their eyes were round, too, except when their smiles squeezed them into crescent moons. With their small noses and mouths, they looked like a pair of innocent kids.

The woman was a computer engineer, and would often work overtime and arrive late. Then her fiancé was on his own. He didn't take the initiative to pair with any of the single girls – i.e. with me – because his partner would soon be there. I didn't take the initiative, either, not at first. But one day, another day on which Princess had left me stranded, I got up the courage to do just that. I walked over to him, offered him my hand, and gave him my best shall-we-dance smile. We stepped forward, to the side, back, to the side, advancing and yielding in turn, but mute the entire time. It was just our bodies that were paired, not our souls.

But what a pleasure it was to dance with a partner who knew how to use his body properly. He never jerked me because he was off balance. He didn't sway. He gave me a steady lead, guidance and support. My body gushed with warmth. It was a tingling sensation, almost electric, which I'd only ever felt before with Donny. This guy could approximate the thing that Donny did.

Donny always said that the main thing in Latin is to stay straight and low. You have to turn around your axis and step *deeply* into the floor, to get your centre of gravity as low as you can. Every movement comes from the floor through the core. That's the feeling! That's how you use your body, whether you're a woman or a man.

A man who uses his body correctly doesn't need to control the woman's body; he just has to give her clear directions and she will respond beautifully. You shouldn't have to force it. No, you can't force it.

Dancing with that guy felt effortless. It was so good I felt like crying.

His fiancée showed up in the middle of the third piece of music. I bowed out as soon as I saw her. Smiling, she took her future husband's hand and he danced her into the crowd. He was smiling now, too. Her name was Meixin. His name I can't recall. But he was a good dancer, and they seemed a fine match.

Height-wise, and height is the most obvious initial consideration, the best match is for the man to be 10 to 15 centimetres taller than the girl, so he can lift his arm high enough for her to do an underarm turn without having to duck. That's hard when he's the same height, let alone when he's shorter and his partner is wearing heels. I'm almost 165 centimetres in socks, well over 170 in heels. It was going to be hard for me to find a partner among the gentlemen in the group class who was tall enough. The guys in the studio were in their prime, and hyper-competitive. Everyone there was looking for a partner that could add to his score and raise his ranking. They'd never consider me, no matter how matched we might be in stature.

How I longed to meet my match! I wanted to climb higher, to reach my peak. I was desperate for a steady partner who belonged to me. When I found him, if I ever did, we'd get to know each other, body and soul.

3

RECONSTRUCTIVE SURGERY

The first time my cousin tried to kill himself, my mother took me to visit him in the hospital.

On a Sunday afternoon near the end of a weekend's leave from his mandatory military service, he'd locked himself in the bathroom and knocked back a bottle of Drāno Liquid. He was rushed to the hospital, where the doctor grafted a section of his colon into his throat, to reconstruct his oesophagus.

The day we went to see him he was in the post-op ward. He couldn't eat or speak. He had a long road to recovery ahead of him, and would probably be in there for a couple of months.

It was scorching hot that day, and windless. After getting jostled around in the back seat of the taxi for the longest time, I felt stifled and dazed.

Auntie met us in the hallway outside and beeped us in.

My mum started talking as soon as she stepped into the room. She took it upon herself to guide Cousin through his rough patch, because in my mum's humble opinion Auntie was too mild-mannered to say what needed to be said, and because she was a widow. If my mum didn't say it, nobody would. She thought it was her duty to bring her elder sister's wayward son back on track – especially since she'd helped take care of him so many times when he was a baby.

But all Mum did was preach. She didn't console, she exhorted, with an endless stream of advice. She was going to give a kid who'd lost his will to live a correct understanding of life. The doctor had reconstructed his oesophagus. My mum knew all about that, but ever since she'd dropped out of pre-med to marry my dad, she had taken on a different role in life: she was going to reconstruct my cousin's mind. My mum believed that any failure in life was due to lack of trying. A man who took his life into his own hands like Cousin had must be weak. He must lack willpower. If it wasn't so, then why had his elder sister, who'd had the same family upbringing, got into medical school?

By this point she was really worked up. 'You could make a living as a grease monkey! Even small fry can fight!'

He just lay there, unable or unwilling to respond. He

didn't look at my mum; he looked out of the window. When his eyes settled on me, I met his gaze and smiled, but he just blinked and looked away.

My mum was still giving 'the speech', and because Cousin wasn't paying attention she was getting increasingly dramatic, or histrionic. Auntie had had enough. She took my mum out to have a tea.

Then it was just him and me. I gave him my best friendly, enquiring look. This time he met my gaze and held it.

I walked to his side, taking care not to bump the tubes and wires that were feeding him and monitoring his vital signs, and took his hand.

'People can be so awful. I hate them, too. But someday it'll be our turn. We'll show those bastards, you'll see. Everything's going to be all right. It's just like the lady said: since you survived, you've got to fight!'

My cousin smiled, for the first time since I'd got there, reminding me what a handsome kid he was and how like his mother he looked. They had big eyes, just like my mum, with the creases in their eyelids that many Asians consider attractive. They had prominent noses in narrow, almost delicate faces. They had movie-star features. But they were both short.

His smile disappeared as soon as our mothers came back in. He went back to wearing the same wooden expression.

A few days later, Auntie called to say Cousin wanted to

see me. With the self-righteous concern of a true do-gooder, my mum said she'd go the next day and set him straight.

'No, not you,' Auntie said. 'He only wants to see Summer.'

Mum didn't give me permission. Instead, she went to see him herself, several times. And a lot of good it did him.

After he was discharged from the hospital, he went straight back to the base, where it was more of the same. Or maybe it was even worse now that he'd been so outrageously derelict in his duty. So he did it again – he took another drink of Drano. The doctor gave him another oesophagus. The reconstructive surgery didn't go as well, but this time he'd escaped for good. He spent the rest of his military service in physio and counselling.

After he got home again he tried his third bottle, and as far as I know it was his last. It was also about the last I heard about him. My mother stopped keeping me up to date. I never made the effort to reach out. I assumed he wanted to be left alone.

He hasn't attended a single family gathering since – not that there have been many to attend. We all live in the same city, but like a lot of city clans we don't have much to do with one another. Whenever there's a get-together, whatever the occasion, I usually say I'd love to come but I'm busy. But my cousin apparently flat out refuses, every time.

Cousin is still living at home. His sister moved out when

she got married, so it's just the two of them there now, widow and son.

It's been over twenty years, but I often think of him, how cute he used to be, and what he might look like today. Sometimes I imagine him with an unkempt beard. And he's very thin. He's getting old, just like me.

It's not bad to be old; it's actually good, as it gives you a chance to reflect. Lately I've been collecting memories and trying to string them together, like pearls on a necklace. They often don't seem significant at first, but if I think of something it might be a clue to one of the many riddles of my adult life. Is it better to unravel these mysteries? Maybe not. But on the whole I think it is good to understand. Understanding doesn't necessarily bring happiness; it might leave you deeper in sorrow. But at least now I can see that the sorrow isn't just in me, it's in my family. Maybe it's in the human condition, in the blooming and withering in a person's life.

It saddens me to realise that. But having reached the realisation, having made it this far in life, something tense inside has finally relaxed a bit, and loosened up. I hope my cousin feels the same way.

One of my mother's photos is creased and faded with age, but the girl in the photo is still just as beautiful. Her hair is swept back from her clean, bright face. She is sitting in a white dress with a violin and a bow on her lap. She was about to give a recital. The photographer came to the house.

That was her well-off, bright and beautiful girlhood, which she was so proud of and which didn't include me.

If only my mum had remained a girl for ever, without ever having to grow up. The same goes for me. Maybe the world would be a happier place if none of us ever developed secondary sexual characteristics and the ability to reproduce. In that kind of pre-pubescent world, my mum would have been happy, I'd have been happy. Who knows? I might even have been loved.

My mother once took me to the hospital for a chronic cough and a sinus infection. The doctor said they'd better take an X-ray to check for fluid build-up. The X-ray technician gave me a gown to go and put on. My mum stopped me on the way to the changing room.

'What do you think you're doing?'

'I have to take my shirt off, put this on and wait for them to call my number.'

'You have to take your shirt off?'

'Yeah.'

'You're not allowed to take your bra off.'

'But he said I have to, that's how they take the X-ray.'

'No, you don't. You can't. What, you want to be a stripper?'

I wasn't sure what that was supposed to mean, or who I should listen to. In the end I obeyed my mother. I put the gown on over my bra and went in.

'Hey, you're wearing an undergarment,' the technician said through the microphone from the other side of the Plexiglas.

I blushed and nodded.

'Please go back to the changing room, take it off and come back.'

I was led out by a nurse assistant. My mum asked if they'd taken it. I shook my head. 'The guy said I had to take my bra off.' My mother was stony-faced.

I hurried into the changing room, took off my bra, draped the gown over my shoulders and ran back into the X-ray room.

I got the sense that my mother despised my body, and that she wanted to control it, too. And what did my body mean to her? To her, my body meant my gender, and my gender signified sex.

My health wasn't actually that important to her, and she didn't care about what was on my mind, about what I was thinking. I can't blame her, in retrospect. Few of the people I met later on cared about those things, either. To a lot of people, especially most men, I am my body, and my body is a sex object.

Sex I could mostly do without. For most of my life, sex

has seemed like a form of violence, inseparable from other kinds of domination. Sometimes I have put up with it. But I almost never want it. I've almost never needed it.

What I needed was non-stop nourishment, both physical and spiritual. For a long time, that's all I wanted out of a relationship – cooking and companionship. I was enamoured with men who were good cooks and conversationalists, who would feed me and talk to me. They gave me what I needed; I gave them what they wanted.

I had never had what I needed, let alone wanted, at home, in any sense. My mum used to complain she'd spent half her life cooking meals for me. Inhaling fumes, getting splattered. She always cooked up a bad mood. She'd slam my plate on the table and tell me to hurry up. I could forget about talking or even watching television while I was eating. She'd tell me to chew with my mouth closed and keep my eyes on my plate. It was never 'How does it taste?' It was 'You're still not done yet? How much more of my time are you going to waste?' She never begrudged my father the time it had taken her to make a meal. She'd make his favourite dishes. But I guess I wasn't worth her time. She always reminded me how long it'd taken her to make a meal that I could polish off in ten minutes, leaving no trace of all her hard work apart from dirty dishes, indigestion and shit.

Smart girls don't let themselves wind up in the kitchen,

she would say. Strangely enough, that's about the only life advice I got from her that I ever ended up following.

My relationship with my mum got worse and worse the older I got. She'd criticise me endlessly when I was at home. At school I was distracted, preoccupied with whatever had happened that morning. After school I could look forward to another round of criticism, another full-course dinner of belittlement – and maybe another makeover of my room. My desk might have moved to the other side of the bed, or my bookshelves would all be gone. I might find them on the bathtub, and the books by the toilet bowl. She might have flipped through my notebooks to see if I was keeping a diary. If so, she wanted to see what mischief I was thinking of making. To her, I was ready to misbehave, go off the rails at any time. One time she installed a new wardrobe with a mirror on the door, facing the bed. It gave me a start every time I woke up in the middle of the night, like someone was watching me. I'd get more and more anxious on the way home, wondering what it would be that day.

I had no sense of stability. My room might be different. She might yell at me or give me the silent treatment. By that point, the silent treatment was actually fine by me.

Later, I'd start screaming whenever she opened her mouth to speak, and she'd call my father over to slap me back to my senses. Even later than that I started screaming from the hallway outside our flat, so loud the neighbours heard. My mother would drag me in and accuse me of wanting to air our family's dirty linen.

I didn't know what was so wrong with me. I withered daily. I had nowhere to call home, because my actual home was a scary place. It was a prison where I could never be at peace.

'Why do you keep changing my room?' I got up the courage to ask, once.

'*Your* room? My roof, my room. I can change whatever I want.'

After I'd gone to bed, my mum would come in with a litany of everything she was dissatisfied with. It might be my clothes, my body language, my schoolwork, even my smile.

Being her daughter was exhausting. My head hurt.

'Can't you wait until tomorrow? Or tell me before I'm in bed?'

'Listen, I'm busy. Do I have to accommodate myself to your schedule? You can't take a bit of criticism? It's not like I'm not letting you sleep. When I'm done you can sleep.' When she was done, I found it hard to get to sleep.

Life didn't get any better after I got into college. One day I came home to find a long letter on my pillow. It started out with how much money and time and energy she'd invested in me. She'd had me and raised me, and all I'd ever done was disappoint her. But as my mother she was granting me amnesty, out of concern for my future. She had arranged for a doctor to do a simple procedure called a hymenoplasty, to graft who knows what flap of skin into my groin, to reconstruct my vagina. It was so I could make a fresh start. I was supposed to understand how much she loved me. And that all she wanted was the best for me.

By the time I'd read the flip side of that letter, I'd gone from groaning to screaming. I ran away from home that evening.

I wandered around for a while, and ended up spending the night at a gay friend's place, initially on his sofa, later, just so I could be close to someone, on the floor beside his bed. When I went home the next day my parents were eating brunch. I went into my room to get the letter so I could have it out with her in front of my father, but it wasn't there.

When my father went into his study to get a magazine or something, she proudly said she'd burnt it. 'You think I'd let you keep it and hold it over my head? Not that there was anything wrong with anything I wrote.'

When my father returned to the table my mum started to complain that I was hanging out who knows where, always coming home late or not coming home at all. Afraid of a slap, I fled to my room. 'Summer has probably switched boyfriends again,' I heard her say.

I lay down on the bed and tried to catch my breath. How

could I have become that kind of girl in my mother's eyes? I was a virgin! I'd never been kissed. I was in the bloom of youth, but I felt worn down, worn out. I opened my legs and felt the black, wet hole in my groin. What was so wrong with it? Or with me?

Once I was so distraught that I went to talk to my dad. He had never intervened in conflicts between my mother and me, or been personally involved in my life at all. He was always busy, with his company and his work. Even when he wasn't working, he was preoccupied, off in his own world. He was cold to anyone who tried to invade that world. He wouldn't speak if he was interrupted, he'd just walk away. If he couldn't do that, he would lose his temper.

I was so desperate that I took the risk that he would lose his temper or worse – go behind my back and tell my mother what I'd divulged – out of the hope that he would take my side, or at least see where I was coming from. 'Please,' I begged him. 'Tell her not to treat me this way any more.'

'Her?' he asked.

I couldn't continue.

'Whatever it is, keep me out of it.'

But I guess I'd made some kind of impression on him, because a couple of weeks later he sought me out. He was cool and composed. That was his style.

'I won't object to you moving out,' he said. 'But I don't

plan on supporting you. I'll keep giving you the same allowance every month, no more.'

Having made this announcement, he walked away.

I seriously considered it. I asked a few classmates who'd moved up north to Taipei for college to get an idea of what the rent would be, but realised I wasn't up to it. I'd never had a job; I hadn't a hope of being independent. So I resigned myself to my life – crying, going to class, staring out of the window. I knew nobody was going to appear and pull me out of hell.

Nobody would help me, especially as I didn't look like someone who needed help. I had piano class, art class. I was a good-looking young woman. I wore posh clothes. Anyone would assume that I could just sit there and people would like me. Even if I told people the truth, nobody would believe me.

One Sunday morning I lost it. I hit her. I pushed her and kicked her.

My mother sobbed at the injustice, wild-eyed and apparently shocked. 'I knew you were an addict!'

I lost it again. This time I laughed out loud, so hard my tummy hurt. I threatened to hit her again but she grabbed my arm.

That evening my father made me make a solemn apology. 'What's got into you?' he asked. We were mother and daughter, no matter what. How could I do such a thing?

Now it was my turn to be cool and composed. I walked over to my mother and said it, in a monotone. Then I laughed and left.

Only many years later, after leaving, failing and coming back over and over again, was I able to leave for good. I still felt guilty, somehow, as though I'd abandoned her. But I needed to survive, and to do that I had to get away from her. I felt totally inadequate, but I'd finally escaped.

Lately I've been having a recurrent dream about something that happened in the first year of secondary school.

It's raining in the dream but I don't have an umbrella. I have to walk home in the rain.

It's like I've peed my pants without feeling the need to go. My pants are wet with fluid that has flowed out of my body. Is it physiologically possible for the bladder to release its contents without a person noticing, I wonder? Or maybe it has been raining harder than I realise, and it's all from the rain?

Several girl classmates are walking behind me. When I look back, they're pointing and whispering. One of them, a girl in glasses with big round frames, points at my skirt and opens her mouth to speak, but ends up not saying anything.

'It sure is raining hard!' That must be what she was going to say. I keep walking home.

When I get there I go right into the bathroom and sit on the toilet.

My pleated navy skirt is crumpled on the floor at my feet. It's sopping wet. I notice a pale brown liquid flowing into the drain, and then, on my pants, a wet brown stain.

Gross! What is that, I wonder? Without having peed, I stand up and see that the toilet is full of blood, and I can feel the blood trickling down my inner thighs. Soon it forms a scarlet pool on the white tiles.

Ah, it's come, I finally realise.

That was the first time I got my period.

4

MAKING WAVES

There'd been a lot of scuttlebutt around the studio about something that had happened the week before. There'd been an incident at a competition held by a studio in southern Taiwan.

I'd heard rumours about how such one-off competitions were organised – off the local annual dance circuit. One studio might send a representative to another studio to invite the founder to send their best dancers to ensure that the competition would be watchable and give it a veneer of credibility. If the founder of the other studio agreed, it was as if they'd given their blessing, and the competition would almost certainly go off without a hitch. But there were stories of major studios that had refused to attend, publicly doubting the organiser's impartiality or the calibre of the judges, as if the quality of dancing didn't matter at a competition like that. When that happened, the would-be impresario pretty much had to call it off.

In this case the representative had gone not to another studio but to the municipal government. Or maybe the municipal government had approached the studio. Whoever's idea it had been, it was a long way to go, and a lot of money to spend, for an event that few nationally ranked competitors, let alone international stars, would attend. The competitors who went anyway did so in order to get some much-needed experience.

Competitors started complaining about the judging during the qualifying rounds. The complaint initially was that the judges were – surprise, surprise – playing favourites. Then a coach who'd gone south with the competitors from our studio the day before and spent the evening helping them polish their routines discovered that some of the judges didn't even have a professional dance background. There were personal trainers and officials from the municipal sports administration sitting at the judges' table.

In the end, dancers who might have been contenders at the nationals didn't make it out of the qualifiers, beaten by local novices.

The dancers from our studio, along with other out-of-towners who were in the same boat, felt they'd been made fools of. They'd spent all that money and come all that way when all along the winners had been chosen beforehand.

A coach from another studio yelled that a competitor needed a few thousand hours of training, while any idiot could get a judge's certification for a few thousand dollars.

While the coach from our studio was making a formal complaint to the organising committee, angry young dancers started shoving each other and yelling. A fight broke out. It turned into a brawl.

The coach decided not to wait for a response to his complaint. The organisers had demonstrated how incompetent and unfair they were, and he'd made his point. He took his dancers home.

I asked Donny if such things happened often.

'Studios giving each other informal invitations, or making certain arrangements for their competitors – that kind of thing has a way of happening sometimes, I guess.' After all, the big studios *were* a lot like the mountain strongholds in those old novels about the outlaw world of *jianghu*, a faraway realm of 'rivers' and 'lakes'. A studio founder was like a warrior king, the top dancers like the honour-bound heroes who once banded together to fight under a king's flag. Anything could happen in that kind of world, and a lot had happened over the years in the local ballroom dance world, but a competition that ended in a brawl – well, that was the first time Donny had heard of such a thing.

He shrugged. He thought I was making a big deal out of nothing.

He said it was the same overseas. 'There are influential studios everywhere. You think Blackpool is free from that kind of influence? Think again. The organisers don't have to remind them, the judges already know that the major studios won't send their best pairs if they don't have a chance of placing, or if they feel like they have been passed over one too many times in the past. Being cold-shouldered by a major studio would take the shine off even Blackpool, because the elite competitors that represent the studios are the shining stars of any competition. And as stars, they don't just shine, they also attract. They're the draw, the gravity that gets the out-of-towners who fly economy to show up, from around the world for some competitions. You think most of those people have a chance at winning, no matter how good they actually are? No way. They're the rank and file, the also-rans. They're there to make the champions look good.'

'Then why do you bother saving up all that money every year to go to Blackpool?' Making the annual pilgrimage to Blackpool, Lancashire, the mecca of competitive ballroom dancing, with his partner was Donny's main goal in life.

'The system's not entirely rigged, no matter how influential a certain studio might be. And win or lose, I still get the chance to dance while the whole world might be watching. I know we're unlikely to stand out. How can we when we're surrounded by all those Europeans and Americans? Riccardo Cocchi is five foot seven, but he's an

exception. Bryan Watson is well over six feet. We diminu-
tive Taiwanese competitors can show our teeth and claws,
strut our stuff, dance our hearts out, right in front of their
eyeballs, while the judges, however fair they might be,
haven't even noticed that we exist.

'And what other choice do I have?' Donny said.

Donny saw Susan as his best chance to take Blackpool by
storm. Susan came from a ballet background, and had a
degree in physical education. She was lithe and strong. She
used to be his student; now she was his partner.

Once, while Donny was correcting my posture in the
studio, a beautiful young dancer walked into the room.
That was Susan. A small competition was coming up.
They'd arranged to practise after my class.

Donny and I had been laughing and talking like old
friends, but he fell silent the moment Susan made her
appearance. He couldn't take his eyes off her as she
removed her sweatshirt, got a sandwich out of her backpack and chatted with a classmate. When she rapped the
guy on the forehead with her knuckles, Donny looked like
a jealous lover. When the class was over, my time was up
and Donny dropped me, just left me there, and rushed over
to where Susan was sitting. He knelt there in front of her
like an earnest suitor.

On second thoughts, he went to the coffee machine to

make her an espresso, which he carried over on a tray with saucer, cream and sugar, like a waiter. She tried the coffee and said it was too hot. He tested it, his lips at the mark her lips had left on the cup. When the temperature was right, he handed it back to her.

Two people drinking out of the same cup, like in an ultra-romantic *shōjo* manga.

And that wasn't all. While she was trying to fit the laces through the tiny holes in her golden, high-heeled dance shoes, Donny brushed her hand away and laced them for her. Then he lifted her calves over his thigh, put the shoes on her and tied the tips in a bow.

Donny would do anything for her, at least for the chance to dance with her.

He needed a partner to help him fulfil his dream.

Maybe Susan could help him do that, but they weren't exactly a match made in heaven. Susan was a bit tall for him. Actually, not just a bit. She was a big girl, with long legs and fluid lines. If she were a sports car, she'd be a Mustang, while a Mazda Miata might have been more Donny's size and style. Donny accommodated himself to her stature and her aesthetic in the studio and the gym, adjusting the way he danced and adding to his musculature and mass, so that they could stand out on the dance floor with exceptional fluidity and stability. If they had one thing in common, it was speed and strength. When they did the explosive moves in the fast dances, they were stunning, so invigorating and powerful. They were the pair the whole ballroom dancing world in Taiwan had the highest hopes for. They were placing higher and higher in every major competition. At smaller competitions there was no match for them.

The next year they'd go to Blackpool. It was all Donny thought about.

Knowing full well that he had to keep dancing with her if he were to have a hope of competing with the international elite and making a name for himself, he was willing to marry her to keep her. Marriage would make everything a lot easier. The great pairs tend to end up together, as the simplest way to stay together is to get hitched. It's like buying an insurance policy for your dance career. It was what Donny called 'the way of the world'.

'I'll do anything she wants,' he said, 'anything a heterosexual man would do, except go to bed with her and father her children. She can go and fall in love with someone else if she wants, just as long as she keeps dancing with me.'

He needed a good partner to be able to shine on the dance floor. Those were the rules.

Another of those rules was that the gentleman pays. And pays and pays. Donny paid for everything – transportation, lodging, food and costume design. When they took a masterclass Donny took care of the tuition. And if they got a corporate contract he gave the proceeds to her.

'Cash, I need cash,' he used to say with a strenuous smile, by way of greeting.

To get it, Donny had to be resourceful. During the day he worked in the legal office of a pharmaceutical company, and he taught all the evening and weekend classes he could. He even took costume design cases. He stayed passionate about teaching regular students like me and the aunties and uncles, but his passion had a hard-headed, pragmatic edge, because Donny knew he had to keep his eyes on the prize – Blackpool. To get to Blackpool he had to keep his rich lady students satisfied. As far as I could tell he'd managed to do so without compromising his dignity as a dancer.

Grateful that he kept teaching me when the rich ladies brought in more in a week than I did in a month, I redoubled my efforts. Every evening I watched the videos of the famous competitors that Donny had given me so I could refine my footwork. The one I found the most helpful was the basic rumba video Slavik Kryklyvyy had made with Karina Smirnoff. Their movements, and their explanations, were so crisp, clear and clean. I followed along, over and over again. Donny was surprised the next time he saw me. 'How'd you get so good so quickly, girl?' he asked. 'It's all down to Karina,' I said. 'Ah,' he said. 'So that's what you needed, a more mechanical, paint-by-numbers approach. You know, step one, step two, step three.' I stuck my tongue out at him. But it was true: I practised like a machine. I'd put myself on autopilot and lose track of time. On several occasions it was dawn before I put the computer to sleep and put myself to bed.

To celebrate the progress I had made, and to cement it, or for whatever reason, Donny invited me to accompany him to Singapore to watch a WDC competition. The WDC is the World Dance Council, one of the two main dance bodies. The other is the WDSF, the World DanceSport Federation. The WDSF is pro and the WDC amateur. But don't assume the WDC is just for amateurs. All the elite dancers are professionals. Which body you belong to depends on your teacher and the development strategy you're following. I couldn't care less which was which, as long as the dancers were good.

Donny wanted me to see the top international competitors in action. I'd only been able to watch their videos, but now I could see them in person. Donny said this kind of learning was the fastest and most direct.

As on the dance floor, so in daily life, Donny's movements were quick and sure. He booked a package deal – flight and hotel, three days and two nights. He reserved the tickets for the competition. Our schedule was simple. We were there to watch and learn, but would have a day at the end to see the sights.

Then Donny's teacher, the founder of the studio, overheard us talking about the trip. 'Are you doing this according to protocol?' he asked Donny, interrupting us. 'Does she have that much money? Or have you switched partners again?'

'What protocol?' I asked after the founder had left.

'Well, let's just say there are some customs to follow, kind of like a set of additional rules for partner dance. But they don't apply to me and you. I'm not teaching you to pay the bills, so we don't have to follow those other rules.'

'Tell me about them.'

Simple, he said. If a teacher takes a student to observe a competition, she's supposed to pay for everything, and if she's conscientious she'll have a red envelope ready, because the teacher has made the time for a field trip that could have been spent doing something else. If the teacher and student enter a pro-am competition or give a performance, it's the same.

I was taken aback. It was as though the deck were stacked against me, in more ways than one. I was fated to follow my partner's lead, and I wasn't rich. This wasn't a sport for poor girls like me.

'Don't worry,' he said, tousling my hair. 'I told him you and me are friends. It's not teacher and student. We're going Dutch.'

*

We got to the hotel that was hosting the event and found the venue, an immense dance floor with a row of tables for spectators along one side, like towels on a beach beside a shining parquet sea. Donny sat at one-of the tables, as excited as a little girl about to make a sandcastle. He immediately struck up conversation with the willowy older white woman sitting next to him. He seemed so eager to talk to her that I worried he might seem a bit ingratiating, even impolite. But then she seemed to do most of the talking.

Donny leaned over and whispered that the woman was the mother of a Latvian competitor who was third in the amateur ranking. He and his partner were young and beautiful, and they were up next. The mother had been as eager to tell Donny all about her son as he had been to talk to her. The son wanted to keep dancing, but she'd insisted on a traditional career. He had to have something to do after he retired from dancing. He would start his law degree the following September.

I didn't care about the beautiful mother or her talented son. All I remember is that she was eyeing the tailoring of my little black open-back dress.

After the dancers came on and started making waves, I forgot all about her, and Donny. All I had eyes for was the passion that was flooding the floor. Pairs of beautiful dancers of all different skin colours had the same toothy grins, the same stylised expressions. One moment they seemed to be about to eat each other raw, the next they were in a ceremonial procession, and then they were like innocent kids gazing up at the stars. They all had the same heavy makeup, bare shoulders and backs, gold powder and glitter, and fake tans. And they were all sweating so profusely that their costumes were soon sopping wet. If you looked carefully, you might catch a glimpse of the beads of sweat on all those beautiful bodies refracting the light into so many tiny rainbows.

Seeing these fantastical creatures so close up brought tears of rapture to my eyes – what with the seemingly instinctive cries when they unleashed their limbs, the costumes covered in sequins like the sparkling scales of a mermaid and the otherworldly smiles.

When the initial peak of excitement had passed I reminded myself to watch and learn. I couldn't help feeling pleased with myself for knowing what to look for. All that people who don't understand pair dance see is two people holding hands and tracing forms on the floor like a botanical illustrator limning flowers on a page. Maybe they'll pay particular attention to the dancers' extravagant hand gestures, their hand styling? Green spectators tend to do that. But if you've studied dance, you know that what goes on below the waist is more important. Life is the same, strangely enough. When you feel like you're at sea, the best thing to do is look down and plant your feet on solid ground.

Another thing you know to observe if you've studied dance is how the leader leads and how the follower follows. The leader invites with his lead hand, usually in a clear and timely manner, but he can decide not to telegraph the next step until the last possible second, keeping the follower on her toes. However long he takes, there is always a momentary delay between lead and follow, between signal and reception, between invitation and interpretation, which the follower manages, by a million muscular adjustments, to translate into a viscous flow of movement, going forward and back like a precision pulley, or spooling out and in like a yoyo. What happens in that moment is the essence of partner dance interplay. You've got to grasp it for yourself, and you can only do that if you find a truly good dance partner. Then, like the WDC judges sitting at their table on the other side of the dance floor from us, with what appeared to be the subtle smiles of the Buddhas of Angkor Wat on their faces, you can see that understanding in others.

The only thing scheduled for the morning of the second day was the pro-am competition, the one for teachers and their students. It was terrible.

'So these are the rich ladies you were telling me about?' I rolled my eyes.

'Yup. You see why it's scheduled first thing in the morning on the last day of the competition. And why they don't sell tickets.'

We had the day to ourselves. Donny had decided we'd go to the oceanarium, around Sentosa, then up Orchard Road.

Donny was like a model boyfriend, stopping with me at the various displays, taking my photo – one with me and the sharks, another with me and the angel fish – buying me an ice cream cone. We had fun at the beach. He swatted away the sand on my legs. When he treated me to shrimp for lunch, he peeled them for me, afraid my hands would get dirty. He piled them on his plate. When I went to pick one up with my chopsticks, he told me to wait a bit, he was going to warm them in the pot before he'd let me eat. And he'd only let me eat if I'd let him feed me. When he did that he seemed less like a model boyfriend and more like a parody of machismo.

In the afternoon, we walked the two miles from the Dhoby Ghaut Green to the Forum Shopping Mall, and headed back down the other side. It was a whole other world, the turf after a morning of surf. I slipped into boutique after boutique while he waited outside in the hot sun. After several hours of this, I finally asked, 'You're actually tired and bored, aren't you?' Donny just smiled, a smile so practised that it didn't seem the least bit forced.

So Donny had succeeded in moulding himself into

the perfect gentleman, or rather the demands of the male dancer's role had spilled over into the rest of his life. On the dance floor he had to be able to adroitly steer his partner away if someone was going to invade her space; off the dance floor he would patiently, or indulgently, chaperone her, because she might need his protection. But did he really think that the traditional gender logic he'd acquired from dance was the principle behind the division of labour, emotional or otherwise, in a friendship that happened to be between a man and a woman?

I decided to call an end to it, to the walk up and down Orchard Road and to the drama we were acting out. I didn't want a chaperone, or a boyfriend; I wanted a friend. If we were really friends, we shouldn't have to follow the traditional etiquette. As friends we should treat each other as equals, being equally understanding and sensitive to each other. He didn't have to imitate the code of gallantry he had internalised just because I happened to be female.

Well, *I* was tired and bored, I announced. I wanted to sit down and have another bite to eat. But I would be feeding myself.

Over an early dinner we got to talking about the protocol he'd mentioned, and how that meshed with the old-fashioned patriarchal gender norms that underpinned the rumba and the other dances, especially the paso doble. I revealed that when the founder of the studio had asked about the nature of Donny's relationship with me in such a contemptuous tone, I hadn't just been intrigued, actually I could barely breathe. I'd been disrespected! I felt angry all over again. Donny told me to calm down. When I did he gave me a lecture. 'Have some respect,' he said. For one thing, as Donny's teacher, the founder was my teacher's teacher. For another, he was a trailblazer, both he and his wife. I might have a totally different impression of ballroom if not for people like them. I was only interested in ballroom because of people like them.

There weren't many teachers in his teacher's generation, he explained. They'd had to make a lot of sacrifices, and take a lot of risks, for dance.

It used not to be so easy to dance in Taiwan, you know. Before the mid-1980s, there was a Dance Ban, one of many ways that the Kuomintang regime tried to control people's minds and bodies under martial law. When people talk about martial law, they usually have political repression in mind, but restrictions on the body were part of it, too. You couldn't say what you wanted or move your body as you wished. Your blood was free to pulse through your veins – the Kuomintang could hardly ban that – but you weren't free to move your limbs in certain ways. Dance wasn't a healthy expression of bodily instincts, or part of normal social interaction. In addition to being illegal, dance was supposedly licentious and harmful to the social order.

At the time the dance halls, to which the authorities turned a blind eye, were all touchy-feely affairs off Linsen North Road, one of the local red-light districts. The pairs of dancers would join hands and sway their bottoms to the music. The man was a customer, probably a businessman with a gut, and the woman was a hostess, who didn't just dance but also lit cigarettes, sang karaoke, poured drinks, giggled, made small talk and ran her fingers habitually through her hair. Women like that were shameless flirts, as were the men who patronised them. Dancers were degenerates.

At the time, most people couldn't tell the waltz from the cha-cha or the chicken. No matter what kind of dance it was, it couldn't be good.

But even during martial law, at a time when defiance of the Dance Ban, or any kind of protest, could get you interrogated, maybe tortured, maybe even imprisoned if not executed, there were young people who liked dance so much they were willing to take the risk. They came in contact with ballroom dancing through a forbidden book or magazine, and fell in love with it. The only way to study it was to go abroad, which wasn't so easy in those days. As well as the expense, there were a lot of background checks. But Donny's teacher and his wife had found a way. They'd made the pilgrimage to Blackpool, where they had lived for years, on the coast of the Irish Sea.

By the time they got back to Taiwan, dance was legal.

The Dance Ban had been lifted, along with martial law. Dance was still looked down on, though, especially ballroom. But at least by now society was a bit more open, and a studio could make a go of it if it offered classes in ballet and folk, dance forms that sounded somehow more elegant or authentic. They hired teachers to teach such classes, but all anyone really cared about was the rumba and the other Latin dances.

Over the years they did all they could to improve ballroom's local image, just as Vernon and Irene Castle had 'refined the Foxtrot and classed up the Tango', as a dance historian in New York City put it, when they founded Castle House on Madison and 46th Street. Donny's teacher and his wife didn't just found the Fortress, the first dance studio in Taiwan, they also founded the local ballroom association. They held competitions, they taught classes for college dance clubs, they went on television, they wrote newspaper columns. They were ambassadors for ballroom. They were as famous in local dance circles as any hero in *Outlaws of the Marsh*. Their exploits were the stuff of Taiwanese ballroom legend.

Their only regret was that they'd never had a child. That was the choice they'd made. They would have had to sacrifice three years from their careers, and of all the risks they had run mastering the art, that was the one they felt they couldn't afford to take. Ballroom was their baby.

The second-most eminent pair of Taiwanese ballroom dancers, and the founders of the second-oldest studio, learned a lesson from the pioneers – that a dance career can't handle the interruption of pregnancy and childbirth. So they planned ahead. They got married young and she got pregnant before he started his mandatory military service. By the time his service was over, his son was old enough for Grandma and Grandpa to babysit, and he and his wife could continue where they had left off. They were still attending competitions, but their role now was more to promote the discipline at home and abroad. They were planning for their son to inherit the studio.

'What about your teacher's studio?' I asked. 'Will he leave it to you? You're his protégé.'

Donny shook his head. 'Are you kidding? Even if he was ready to call it quits, which he isn't, nobody would hand over a profitable business for free to someone who wasn't family. I'm not family, in any sense. And they don't really approve of the way I live my life.'

I wondered if he meant hanging out with a student like me who wasn't his girlfriend, or other breaches of protocol that he might not be comfortable talking about, even with a friend like me.

'Let's just say,' Donny said, 'I wish my colleagues at the pharmaceutical firm would be a bit nicer to me.' He tilted his head down and opened his eyes wide, giving me his inimitable meaningful look. It was a little like he was glaring at me. He looked kind of fierce. 'Actually, I think they're envious of me.'

'Huh?'

'Because I'm a dancer. In addition to my job, I've got dance. They don't.'

'Do they know you dance? Do they know where you go every day after work?'

'They don't. I wouldn't want them to! But I imagine they can sense that I've got a world outside the office that they know nothing about. Just the secret I've got should be enough to make my ordinary co-workers envious.'

I asked him if he wanted to quit his job and focus on dancing and teaching.

He shook his head again. 'No way! I'd be selling my body.' Donny said he'd seen too many cases of dancers who quit their jobs to pursue their careers, and hadn't lasted that long. 'Passion doesn't pay the bills. Pretty soon you lose all that's left of your purity. You start drumming up business, putting price tags on people, figuring out who can pay and who can't. If I had to support myself teaching dance, I'd become another kind of person.'

He said he didn't want to test himself. He didn't want to test human nature.

*

When we got back to the hotel, Donny went to the exercise room. I didn't want to go out. I just wanted to take it easy.

Donny was gone a long time. He must have made a friend. I could just chill.

Well, I was chilling out when I noticed the black hoop of fabric on the floor between our beds. It had been there the night before. A cotton-Lycra mix, I assumed, but I couldn't be bothered to check. Must have been Donny's sock. I went to the bathroom twice, stepping around the hoop thing both times.

Then I decided to take a shower. Why not a bath? I thought.

I was soaking in the tub when I heard a knock at the bathroom door. An insistent one. I wrapped a towel around me and opened the door. Donny was standing there holding that black hoop on his index finger.

'Yours.'

'It's your sock!'

'It's yours!' he said, dumping it in my hand.

In a huff, I unrolled it. Oh shit, it was a pair of my socks. Ashamed and angry, I slammed the door in his face.

As I learned when I went out, Donny hadn't just gone to the exercise room. Sitting at the pec dec, he'd made a friend who'd taken him to a little bistro around the corner, where Donny had made eyes and small talk with a cute waiter.

There aren't any nightclubs to go to around here – where do you young people go after hours?

It had gone something like that.

Later that evening, Donny said he was going out again, and not to wait up for him. I nodded, expressionless. I watched some TV and went to sleep. I didn't notice when he got back.

5

PAIRING PROBLEMS

Most men are fine with leading their partners, as Donny was trying to do when he took me to Singapore, for the same reason they're fine with patriarchy. Some of them aren't as nice as Donny about it, though.

Like the short chef who danced with a pasty-faced civil servant in the aunties and uncles class. He had a high opinion of himself and was always telling others what they were doing wrong, especially his partner. I noticed she always nodded, but not because she actually agreed with him. She just understood his temper. If she wanted to get along with him she had to submit.

Then again, it wasn't always the girl who had to submit. More than once I'd seen Mrs Lai, the queen bee of the aunties and uncles class, chew out poor old Mr Lai, even though often it was her fault. She'd yell at him no matter what. Her husband might lead, but she wore the pants on and off the dance floor.

There was another such pair, Meixin and her fiancé, who were taking a two-on-one class with Donny at the studio. Donny was helping them prepare for a competition. They were in the time slot before mine. When I came early I'd watch them practise. When Donny showed the fiancé how to do something, Meixin often came over and sat down on the bench beside me. It narrowed the distance. We hadn't ever talked in group class.

They seemed a good match; they were always smiling, and they even looked alike. But when they started dancing she could be pretty demanding, even rude. She would yell at him for the smallest misstep. She appeared to have a strong personality.

So it seems like pair relationships, whether the pair are dance partners, lovers, teacher and student, husband and wife, parent and child, tend towards cruelty and violence as a general rule.

That doesn't make being alone any easier. In fact, there's nothing worse.

I thought only someone as clumsy as me – a meatfoot, as we say in Taiwanese – would suffer alone, unable to find a partner. But the world's best dancer, and my favourite, Joanna Leunis, did too, not to mention Bryan Watson, the reigning king of Latin at Blackpool. And so did Slavik Kryklyvyy, whose videos I used to stay up late watching.

Some of these stars were abusive, but that wasn't necessarily the reason they were alone.

Whatever the reason, it was about to happen to Donny, too. He'd set his heart on Susan. He wanted her to be his partner in dance, and even in law. But Susan obviously didn't feel the same way. She wanted to graduate from college and have another sort of life. Sure she could dance. But she didn't care that much about it. Her plan was to get her physical education teacher's certificate, get married, have a family, be domestic.

Donny said she'd started to avoid him, making up excuses not to come and train. She would come late, and wouldn't take his calls.

'Has she found another partner?'

'Not another dance partner – she's fallen in love. She's crazy about the guy. I bet she takes his calls.'

He'd seen her once, waiting for the light to change. She was riding on his scooter, her arms wrapped around his waist, her cheek against his back. She must have seen him and heard him call her name, but she pretended she hadn't.

The light turned green and they sped off.

'She's a good dancer,' Donny said, fuming. 'With me, she could make it internationally. We could do really well. After all I've done for her, she ditches me, for a man, for love. What's so great about love? Is love a reason not to dance?'

'Phys ed majors are so brainless!' he exclaimed a few minutes later. 'What else does she have but a bit of talent for dance? What other way is she going to be able to shine in this lifetime? By getting married and working part-time as a substitute teacher?'

Isn't that what you were planning to do – marry her? I thought, but stayed silent, to spare his feelings. And your reason for marrying her wasn't love, it was your dance career. It didn't sound like a very good reason to get married.

'Dance is what you want to do in life,' I finally said, 'but it's obviously not what she wants. What's wrong with that? What's wrong with a girl who can dance but doesn't want to, a girl who just wants to fall in love and get married?' It was painful for me to say.

Donny was too angry to reply. Quite a few minutes passed before he took a deep breath and shrugged.

'I'd really marry her, you know,' he finally said. 'I'll support her. She can keep dating her boyfriend behind everyone's back, I don't care. That's not something I can give her. I don't want to, either. All I want to do is dance. I just want her to keep being my partner, that's all. I really don't care.'

'She cares.'

*

After breaking up with Susan, Donny held a lot of tryouts. Some girls lasted a few months, but he kept switching. One of them had big eyes, a big mouth and dark skin. When I had an individual class with Donny she'd come too. Sometimes when I just couldn't get it, Donny would demonstrate with his partner, who would do it effortlessly. Why can't I? One time she arrived with a reddish-orange practice dress – for me. That was the last time I saw her.

Donny said he'd broken up with her because she would show up without a bra on. He couldn't stand it. 'She should know better, regardless of whether or not she knows I'm gay.' He told her how he felt: disrespected and embarrassed, especially during the rumba. The next time she came wearing a sports bra.

That still didn't cut it. 'Same difference!'

Then he tried out an exquisite doll-like girl. He was completely satisfied.

'She's got the basics down pat,' he said excitedly. 'And she's the right height. I've got a good feeling about this.'

She actually had a lot in common with Donny, including ambition. She had a dance partner, and they'd got engaged. Then the guy said he needed to be by himself for a while. They'd started dancing for fun, but now they were going to a lot of different competitions, ingratiating themselves with VIPs, identifying who might be Mr or

Mrs Moneybags, so that when the boss gave them a quota they could sell enough tickets at ten thousand a chair, a hundred thousand a table. Now they had a quota to make and a lot of other things to do.

The guy said it had become too competitive and polit-ical. He wasn't in it for fame or profit. It wasn't for him.

So he'd asked her to give him some time to think it over. During the break she could dance with someone else. If he decided to quit, she could dance with whoever she wanted. But they'd get married no matter what.

That was part of why Donny was so excited. If the guy decided not to dance, he wouldn't be too picky about Donny teaming up with his fiancée, because of Donny's sexual orientation. Problem solved, it seemed.

But there was a bigger problem: the girl was a dancer at another studio, which meant that she was a heroine who had made a name for herself at another mountain stronghold. Mountain strongholds weren't supposed to headhunt each other's heroes in *Outlaws of the Marsh*, nor were studios supposed to poach each other's top prospects. It wasn't written down anywhere. It didn't need to be said. It was a matter of protocol.

Donny wanted to dance so much that he asked the girl to persuade her teacher to let them break with convention. A bit like *Romeo and Juliet*, but for the sake of dance.

It wasn't going to happen.

So he kept holding tryouts but failing to find a suitable partner. He was on edge.

Around the same time I saw a TV documentary set in Wuhan, China.

It was about a man with Down's syndrome who fell in love with ballroom dance. He didn't have a partner, but he liked the idea of partner dance so much that he registered for classes at all the dance studios in the city. And every teacher would say the same thing: practise by yourself for now, and keep practising until you've mastered the basics. As long as you keep at it, as long as you don't give up, you'll find a partner, someone who's right for you, someday.

In every country, city and studio, there's a dance teacher who will say the same thing. It's the kind of vapid advice you get from a typical relationship expert. When pairing problems arise in any human society, you hear it: that if you try hard enough, your other half will appear, and if they don't you can't really have been trying. You would have found them if you had kept the faith.

People who have really practised ballroom know that what these teachers say is a lie, because there are some basics that one person cannot practise alone. Nobody will tell you that, when you're first starting out, for mercenary reasons. They just want you to keep paying the fee. They hope you won't ever find out.

Like the man in the documentary. He kept it up for ten years.

I watched the footage of him dancing alone, an expression of love on his pockmarked face. He did one person's steps, imagining that the circle had been completed, that he was holding a real live partner in his arms, when all he was holding was air.

To me it was frightening. He was in earnest, a look of rapture on his face, ribcage up, shoulders back, head high. For a decade he'd been embracing a partner who didn't exist.

He had a job as a caretaker but everything in his life was oriented around dance. In one of the interviews he looked right into the camera and said: 'I'll keep working on the basics, I'll keep looking for her. If I can't find her, I'll just wait. She'll appear when the time is right. No matter what, I won't give up.'

At some point, his story had got out. MAN WITH DOWN'S WALTZES ALONE was the headline to the local news story that went viral. A lot of people read about him, including the director of the documentary. But nobody came to try out with him, at least not at first.

Of course, he knew why.

He wasn't good-looking, not at all. But it wasn't just his features. He also looked somehow proud, even full of himself. There was something frightening about the look in his eyes. It wasn't passion for dance, it was an overactive imagination, it was clinging to the idea of a partner, and it was bigger than ballroom.

Eventually the man found someone who wanted to partner with him, a woman who'd seen his story in the paper and sent a letter to his studio. Her name was Sister Shen, and she was forty-seven years old. She too loved ballroom, against all odds. She was heavy-set and powerfully built. She might have been called handsome, at best, when she was younger. Her day job was washing dishes in a restaurant and doing odd jobs, all for minimum wage. And she spent every spare yuan on dance.

When she read the story in the paper, she felt she could relate. She assumed she knew how he felt. He'd spent over a decade watching people dance the dances he was so desperate to do. The desire to find a partner and the pain of not being able to must have eaten away at him. He must have had to hypnotise himself, to tell himself it wasn't shameful. His outsized desire must have been strong enough, or warped enough, to hold out against the rejection he had met in the world.

Most people would have quit eventually. Anyone else would have been weeded out.

To Sister Shen, they were both disempowered – in the real world and on the dance floor. They should be able to support each other, even cherish each other, if they were able to team up. He would be willing; how could he not be? Mutual understanding would make them the ideal match.

He wrote back telling her to come to the studio for a tryout. After just a few bars he called cut, and told her not to move until he told her to. 'What are you doing dancing before I've even started? You have to wait for my lead!'

It did not go any better the second time. When the music recommenced, she jumped the gun again, and he broke away in irritation. 'Don't you understand how ballroom is supposed to be danced?' he asked. 'It's not bumper cars, you know!'

She looked so embarrassed. She didn't say anything, just pressed straggling hairs against her fat red cheeks and let him excoriate her.

Maybe only I could see what was really going on. Though he was ugly, he begrudged Sister Shen her appearance and her age. It was as if he wasn't just choosing a dance partner, but also a wife. That was what happened to most dance couples, after all: they would become couples in real life. And he wasn't interested. Talk about beggars can't be choosers.

Then came another shot of him talking into the camera, but from close up this time. Off screen, the director asked: 'Do you think you'll keep dancing with Sister Shen? Is she the dance partner you've been looking for all these years?' The man smirked. 'The jury's out,' he said. 'I'll give her a chance. But she'll have to learn to let me lead or it's just not going to work out.'

I finished the documentary, disgusted. I knew that it had, unintentionally, transmitted a truth, and not just about the pairing problems in dance. It was the truth of the world of desire.

I turned off the TV and put on Slavik Kryklyvyy's rumba basics instruction video. It was already dawn. I practised for twenty minutes before giving up and going to bed.

I told Donny I wanted to try dancing with a school student, one of my classmates in the group class.

It was called the aunties and uncles class but, as I said, there were some young people in it, and the youngest was a seventeen-year-old named Youlin. He'd been dancing with his tutor, who'd been taking dance since she was small. *Her* teacher was Youlin's father, who had taught the aunties and uncles class before Donny took over. The tutor had gone on an exchange, and Youlin had started to dance when he felt like it, which wasn't very often. His father was working as a foreman in a factory in Shanghai, but wanted his son to keep dancing, and kept trying to get him to shape up from a distance. Youlin's mother and elder brother were supposed to remind him to attend. Some of the aunties and uncles, who had seen him grow up, were there to see if he showed up, and to keep an eye on him when he got there. That's where I came in. I hoped I had a role to play, too.

I thought I could be his partner. If Youlin was willing to team up, we could work together with Donny and improve by leaps and bounds. We'd get really good.

'Yeah, you would,' Donny said, perhaps just to humour me. 'Youlin's a lump of clay, and I could mould him. If Youlin is up for it, I could do a two-on-one for you at the studio. But you mustn't, under any condition, pay his tuition for him. You've got to make him feel he needs to take a class, that he wants to dance with you, that it's worth his while. If you help him, or serve him, and he doesn't have to pay any price, then he'll look down on you. He'll take all your hard work for granted.'

I said I took the point, I knew where he was coming from. And I did. But of course we were both getting way ahead of ourselves.

There were a few not insignificant problems with our plan.

One was that Youlin was full of himself. He didn't think he had any room for improvement. Maybe he was the worst kind of dancer, the kind who can't see his own problems in the mirror. But I saw. He had a good physique, but he didn't use it as well as he could. His waist was stiff, when the basic requirement for Latin dance is a supple core. He didn't see it, or he couldn't feel it. He had stopped improving.

Another problem was that Youlin didn't have much regard for Donny, because he thought that the only one better than him was his old man, who was better than anyone. His dad thought so, too, even though he wasn't even in the same league as Donny, in my humble opinion. He'd come and watch Donny teach when he was back on vacation, and would even criticise him in front of the class. He was really rude, and so was his son. Youlin would express disagreement, disbelief or even disgust when Donny made certain demands on his dancers. He wouldn't say anything out loud like his father, but you could still tell.

Yet another problem was that I had competition. When I summoned the courage to ask Youlin if he wanted to practise with me, he sized me up, smiling but not really smiling. He didn't look me in the eye. 'All right, I can lead a lot of people, you can be one of them.' He'd given me a floppy nail – an implicit rebuff. But I didn't flinch. As long as he didn't refuse outright I still had a chance. Who knew that Princess, my former friend and partner, would overhear his reply and come over to join the conversation. I thought she'd be angry at me. It turns out I'd really under-estimated her.

'If you can dance with more than one,' she said, 'count me in, take me, too. I want to dance the girl's part. I never enjoyed it when I had to take the lead.'

Youlin's vanity was satisfied. He smiled broadly.

And that's how Princess and I ended up sharing Youlin. We'd take turns dancing with him. He was like a sultan in his harem, enjoying the girls who competed for his affections.

Youlin was super satisfied with the arrangement. At least he was pleased with Princess. She was none too sure on her feet. She still couldn't remember the steps. To Youlin, these were positive qualities. She was relaxed, easy to get along with. She was happy to dance with a young hunk like him. She didn't have an active desire to better herself. She always had a smile on her face, and she thought he was top of the class. She was too much of a neophyte to find any fault with his dancing, and regarded him with affirmation, doting on him like the older sister he never had. She was a good audience for Youlin, and he repaid her with tolerance. He was unfailingly nice to her, warm and polite. He certainly never got angry at her.

I was different. Even though I was technically a much better partner for him than Princess, I was pickier. I knew when he'd made a mistake, such as when he missed the beat or overshot a movement. The one and only time I said anything he got angry at me, letting go of my hand, shaking his head and giving me a nasty look, like the man in the documentary. I'd learned my lesson, that I had to bite my tongue. But I couldn't help noticing, and when I noticed I reminded him that he wasn't quite as good as he thought he was. I let him lead but I refused to submit to him the way that Princess did. At the same time, I knew I didn't have anyone else. Youlin was my only choice – the only one in the class tall enough to dance with me and the only one who was available to dance with me. I had to put up with him in order to have a partner to keep dancing with. Youlin sensed in me a combination of ambition and desperation, and it wasn't to his taste. He just wanted to fool around. So more and more he gave me the attitude. More and more I had to tell myself to grin and bear it. Dance with him as long as you can, I told myself. Maybe fate has something good in store.

Whether it was good or not, something did in fact happen. Contrary to appearances, Princess found sharing Youlin just as hard to take as I did. In fact she couldn't stand it. She couldn't see the point of continuing and stopped coming. Yes! Virtual fist pump. Youlin seemed certain to become my steady partner in group class, as a matter of course.

He didn't acknowledge it. He insisted it was for the time being, that we were just classmates, not partners. There was no unspoken understanding, at least not between him and me. Between me and the aunties and uncles, on the other hand, maybe there was. If he came, they'd smile knowingly at me and make space for him to dance with me. That's how it went for over a year.

During that year he kept coming when he wanted, which was usually late and often not at all. When he didn't turn up I danced on my own, or relied on the kindness of relative strangers, on male dancers whose partners were taking a break or were absent. If someone's partner was late or truant, I'd go over and offer myself. When the late partner arrived, I'd let go of the man's hand. He'd return to his partner's side, and I'd go back to dancing alone, waiting for Youlin.

One day, at the end of class, Youlin announced that his dad was back in Taiwan for two weeks' holiday, and that he wanted to meet me. He wanted to see how good his son's partner was, and whether or not we were suited for one another and meant to keep dancing together – particularly considering that I was Donny's student.

Youlin's eyes were flashing with a mischief that in a few years would turn into commonplace adult nastiness. A proud youth made me a proud request. I couldn't help thinking that his pride wasn't based on a sense of self-worth he had earned; it was an inherited case of bad manners.

I smiled and nodded. 'Sure,' I said.

Youlin arranged to meet me the next Sunday morning on the corner of Nanching West Road in an old neighbourhood in the west end that I don't know very well. I live around Taipei 101; I don't know the older, west end of Taipei City, further west even than Linsen North Road. I was surprised that young Youlin was so familiar with a part of the city that was so much older than him. Nanching West Road had had a heyday, decades before he was born. I imagine he must often come around to the local dance halls, where, according to Donny, his dad would some-times teach.

When, like Youlin's dad, you teach in a dance hall, you avoid having to pay a commission, a portion of the tuition, to the founder of a studio. You just need to buy a ticket to get in. To many in the dance community, that smacked of trying to avoid paying your dues, particularly as dance halls hadn't shaken off the disreputable reputation they had acquired in the era of the Dance Ban as places where the wrong sort of people gathered to get up to who knows what. Under no circumstances would Donny have taught in a place like that. In the turbid light, who could tell if the writhing bodies were teacher and student or part-time lovers? It was a totally different ambiance from the bright studio with open windows in which Donny and me and all those lithe young competitors stretched and practised our basic steps with the determination and perspiration of Olympic athletes.

In the nine o'clock morning sun, Youlin looked like your typical handsome young man: a shirt with some basketball star's number on it; baggy pants; baseball cap. Incredibly, when he saw me at the intersection he smiled, a smile so apparently sincere and warm that it took me aback and put me at ease. Golden light splashed on his face and hair. He looked like a breath of fresh air, lacking the dirty looks and bad attitude that he usually gave me in the aunties and uncles class.

No way I was going to let myself get carried away. I didn't trust him.

Youlin took me down an alley past a western restaurant that had not opened for business yet, a haberdashery and a second-run cinema, then down a lane past a temple and the back door of a bank, where we turned towards another major road. Youlin's dad was standing in the entrance of a commercial building. His elder brother and mother were there, too.

I was shocked. They needed to mobilise the whole family to check out a dance partner?

I couldn't help it, I took half a step back.

I looked up at Youlin, who lowered his head and whispered in my ear: 'Relax. It's a regular family outing, and it's not the first time we've invited a guest. My elder brother often brings a classmate or his girlfriend along.'

I'd actually never been in a dance hall before. I'd had no idea that you might find one in a nondescript building in a quiet, downtrodden neighbourhood on a sunny, breezy

Sunday morning, when most people might go out for eggs Benedict. The only places I'd danced were the studio and the exercise centre. I knew that formal competitions or big performances would be held in hotels or in arenas. I'd only heard of dance halls. I never expected it would be like this.

Youlin's dad was sizing me up. He was staring, actually. With his bushy eyebrows he was a bit unnerving. He grunted in greeting, then he took everyone in. It turned out you had to go downstairs, as the dance hall was in the basement. In the sudden dark, I fancied that I was about to attend a meeting of some secret, underground organisation of religious or political extremists, until I heard the music. We went round a corner and I saw a lot of couples under a mirror ball that sprayed dirty yellow rays of light around the room. Some were dancing, others were adjusting their poses in front of the mirrors that wrapped around the walls. It wasn't actually so different to the studio in that respect, but the dancers, like the aunties and uncles, were a lot older, about the age of Youlin's parents. Youlin, his brother and I were the youngest people in there. We looked as though we'd stumbled on the place by accident.

No, I was the only stranger. Youlin and his brother were obviously familiar faces. They must have come here often with their mum and dad. Indeed, Youlin knew the way to the ladies' room. He took me down a hallway and waited for me outside with a considerateness that was most unlike him.

'Better put on your dancing shoes,' he said when I came out, 'so we can start practising.'

'Pra ... practise? Here?' I asked. 'What are we going to practise?'

'Hurry up, my dad is waiting,' Youlin whispered urgently. 'He'll tell us what to do.'

'And we'll do whatever he tells us to?' I asked, sceptically. Then it hit me. Youlin was a little kid afraid to make a mistake, because his father was there. That's why he was on his best behaviour: he was scared of his dad. He wasn't naughty like a little kid, but like a kid he hadn't developed a sense of how he should treat people in the absence of authority figures.

But there was no time for further psychoanalysis of a person I barely knew. I had to deal with that person's father.

Mr Lin told me to do my basic steps for him. I willed myself to focus on my reflection in the mirror, so I could forget where I was, and forget all these people, especially the Lin family. There was only me. Because it was so dim, the me in the mirror seemed to have blue eyes, like an alien. My hair hung limply down to my shoulders. My face looked thinner and sharper than normal. I nodded at myself in the mirror, as if promising that self that I would never let her down, that we would stay true to each other for ever.

Then I started to walk towards my mirror image, repeating my basic rumba steps over and over.

Mr Lin observed me without comment as I drilled the basics. He didn't praise or criticise. He didn't say anything, until he asked me and Youlin to pair up. Then he had us demonstrate underhand turns, alemanas, cucarachas, natural tops. These were the basic moves of partner dance.

When the next song started, Mr Lin took my hand, taking over from his son. We danced the cha-cha. He wanted to see what I felt like, what I was like to dance with.

He was obviously testing me, but was I not testing him? His sense of rhythm was precise, but he seemed to be in a bit of a hurry. He liked to stay right on the beat, and to add flashy little movements every bar. By now it was a habit. That was a habit Donny kept telling his students in the aunties and uncles class not to get into. It was really low class, according to Donny.

Mr Lin was good at best, I was thinking. How did he get to be so full of himself, strutting around like the top dog? Why did the aunties and uncles in the class have such a high opinion of him? Maybe the most important quality for a dancer to have was self-regard, like a forcefield that bent reality around you and warped people's perceptions. If your forcefield of self-confidence was strong enough, people would assume you must be something special.

Then it was Youlin's turn again. He wanted to see what new sequences Donny had taught me.

Youlin's father watched me and Youlin dancing the sequences, again without expressing approval or disapproval. He just crossed his arms and smirked. He was obviously looking for a bone to pick, but it appeared he couldn't find one.

Youlin, and Youlin's dad and I ended up being the only ones in our ad hoc group to do any dancing. His mother just chatted with some other dancers, carrying herself in a strange, affectedly feminine way. His brother spent the whole time on his phone, but he smiled a lot, including at me. He seemed to be the only normal person in the family, the only one you could have a conversation with.

Finally it was over, and the dance hall was closing. It was time for a siesta. When we walked out of that underground space, the full light of noon was shining right into our eyes. We all had to squint.

It took a moment for my eyes to adjust, and for me to readjust to the reality of the city on a Sunday afternoon.

They took me to an old-fashioned American steakhouse, with enamel plates and plastic water glasses, maybe the same ones they'd used when this kind of place was popular forty years earlier. There was corn stew with pastry lid that I hadn't had since I was a kid.

In contrast to Youlin's father, who observed me in such an intrusive and stifling way, the mother didn't pay attention to me at all. She kept running her fingers through her hair. I couldn't tell whether it was on purpose or just a habit. Every so often she would toss it over her shoulder. She kept adjusting her bare-shoulder blouse with a sweetheart neckline. It was dark purple, matching her mascara. Holding her head up with her palm under her chin, she batted her eyelashes.

'Hey,' she said seductively, in a sexy baby voice. 'What are we going to do this evening?' It was as though she were oblivious to the presence of her sons. Her sons seemed just as oblivious. She must have been like this all the time. The effect was all the stranger because she had a lisp, a pronounced one when she spoke quickly. She was like a character out of a Tim Burton movie, and her husband was, too. They looked ordinary, but when you hung out with them, the barely hidden behavioural tics became impossible to ignore. It made you wonder about their kids.

Youlin's brother was short like his father, but had inherited his mother's looks; like her, he was pale and sensual, if that's the right word. Youlin was tall like his mum, but dark like his dad. Personality-wise, Youlin took after his dad, or was trying to, that was clear, while the brother didn't appear to take after either parent. He fulfilled my initial impression, in fact. He was relatable. He was the only one who made small talk over lunch. He was just trying to be friendly and polite; it wasn't some kind of posture. He was also the only one in the family who didn't dance ballroom.

'I learned a few things from my mum and dad when I was younger, and I can still dance a bit. But I never enjoyed it, and didn't keep it up. Youlin did.' He had a dimple in his left cheek when he smiled. He was really quite handsome – more so than Youlin. 'I tag along when we go out, sometimes I dance with my girlfriend. Salsa's popular with people my age, and my dad loves it. It's our family activity. I'll dance a few numbers with you if you'll come with us to a club sometime.'

'Her basics are solid,' Youlin's dad announced, halfway through the meal. 'And she has a good sense of rhythm.' I gathered he was talking to Youlin, and guessed it was his way of saying he was allowed to keep dancing with me. I was worthy.

After that brief interruption, I went back to chatting with Youlin's brother and observing Youlin out of the corner of my eye. I would have expected him to be relieved, but he looked displeased. He was obviously not happy that his brother and I were enjoying a conversation. He was staring at us – another habit he'd picked up from his father.

Another moment of insight, or at least intuition: Youlin was jealous of his older brother. And why would he be jealous? Maybe because his father didn't love him quite as much? That would explain some things – not that it was an excuse for the way he treated me, for all the faces he'd made at me, for his temper tantrums, for the times he just ignored me.

I wondered if his father's announcement might have some impact on the dynamic between us. He would still be the leader and I the follower, but he wouldn't necessarily always have the upper hand, just because of the rules of partner dance.

One time Donny's studio put on an international competition. The finals, in which all the foreign competitors would be dancing, were held in the evening, but there were qualifiers for different divisions all day long – for amateurs, for student and teacher, even for kids. And there were performances. The founder hoped that Donny's aunties and uncles class would put on some kind of a show during one of the breaks. All my classmates were excited; rehearsals were a blast – for everyone except Youlin. For him it was embarrassing to have to wear the cheap costume they'd bought for the occasion. The plastic glitter kept falling off, like lacklustre confetti. Youlin thought he should be in the competition, not in a line of dance with all these old folks.

He didn't come to rehearsals. The class leader, Mrs Lai, asked me if we were going to take part. I said I'd be there no matter what, but whether I danced depended on Youlin. If he wasn't there, who would I dance with?

Mrs Lai had known Youlin's dad for a long time. She called him and the dad gave the order for Youlin to appear. Youlin worshipped and feared his father. He had to agree, but did so unwillingly. He still didn't come to rehearsals. He said he didn't need to, at the level he was at. He just left me hanging there, dancing with air.

He didn't even come to the dress rehearsal the morning of the competition.

Poor you, the aunties and uncles said. They were angry at Youlin, and said he was a spoiled brat, that his dad hadn't raised him right. He paid the fees late, came late to class, didn't even come to the dress rehearsal! He didn't respect his partner. But what could they do about it?

Half an hour before showtime he finally turned up in a hip-hop outfit. Mrs Lai shooed him into the changing room and told him to hurry up and get ready, I'd been waiting for him all day. He didn't say anything or even look at me. He got changed, then we went on stage and finished the performance together.

When we took the group photo, he put his arm around my shoulder and smiled at the camera, like we were partners. I smiled, too.

Then he took back his arm and his smile, and said, 'I've got to get out of these cheap threads, it's humiliating.'

He didn't come back, but I didn't care. In my costume, I watched the competitors perform on stage. It was just the prelims, but I couldn't even dance in the prelims.

I saw Meixin and her fiancé go on stage, arm in arm. It was their first time dancing in front of an audience.

Then I noticed a girl wearing a tasselled dress of orange and gold. She had the thick black eyeliner of an Egyptian queen, like Elizabeth Taylor in *Cleopatra*, and a tiara encrusted with rhinestones. 'You look fabulous,' she cried, smiling to her companion as she led him on stage. Compared to her uptight rivals, including Meixin, she was gracious and relaxed.

My face flushed and my eyes filled with tears, inexplicably. I watched her all through the performance; in fact I couldn't take my eyes off her. When the competitors were coming down the stairs and I was pushed back by the crowd, I was afraid I would lose sight of her.

I felt a tightness in my throat. Some power drew me to her, as though she were my long-lost elder sister in the sea, as though I'd met her before in Atlantica.

Interlude

THE MERMAID'S TALE

Where do mermaids go if they don't feel like rolling back into the water after a sunbathe on the beach – if they're too tired to swim off trailing bubbles in their wake until they vanish at the margin of sea and sky?

They might do what I did. I went in the opposite direction. I grew legs and proceeded with the resolute, plodding steps of someone who had to consciously learn to walk. I walked until I found myself in the middle of a city. There, I learned a style of life I had never imagined, not even in my wildest mermaid dreams. I was busy, but mostly solitary. When I got too lonely, I learned to dance.

I was quite stiff at first, not surprisingly, especially my legs. But a ballet class was the perfect place for me to open them up. We used to ease into the side splits in a sitting position, leaning forward. I could never bend all the way down, until the teacher came and pushed, stepped, or sat down on my back.

Finally, when my chest was pressed against the floor, she was satisfied. 'Nothing happens naturally in dance,' she said. 'No pain, no gain.'

Later on, after I took up Latin dance, I'd spend at least thirty minutes lying on the floor with my legs against the wall. I'd put my feet up, then let them fall into a V. It wasn't an especially wide V at first, because I'd 'retired' after a brief and unremarkable career in ballet. But it got wider and wider over time. My inner thighs would protest, for a few minutes, but then they would quieten down, and I could get them a bit lower, a bit closer to the floor. This was one of my daily rituals. I did it every evening.

I'd close my eyes and listen to the blood flush through my legs. My hands on my inner thighs, I felt the tension in my tendons and my muscles, almost like a low current of electricity.

I'd open my eyes, flex my calves and my quadriceps, and admire my lower limbs – how toned they had become! I'd done this I don't know how many times before I realised that I'd never examined another body part that I had grown after leaving the sea to pursue a life on land. I didn't just grow legs, but the place in between them, too. There was a pond there, and a tunnel that nobody ever read about in that fairy tale.

I wondered, from time to time, whether there was anyone out there like me. I liked to think there was. In fact, I imagined I had an elder sister from the sea. She didn't dislike me or want anything from me. She was actually a part of me. She was a part of my body, maybe the best part.

Like me, she would remember lying with her mermaid sisters on the sea floor, basking in the blooming sun. In our eyes the sun was like a flower, the petals radiating out from the centre. If the water and wind were right, that flower might start turning, like a gyre.

Like me, she would remember tending her underwater garden. All the mermaids had them. Mine started with a circle, a round bed of seagrass that bloomed bright yellow in the spring. When I had the time I visited shipwrecks with my sisters to hunt for treasures to use as decorations, like the white marble carving of a human youth that I had found, and whose smooth skin I caressed daily, to keep him free of barnacles. At some point a rose-red coral tree grew by his side. Like the branches of a weeping willow, its polyps swayed in the current, brushing over the boy's face, or rising and falling like a melody. I sometimes fancied the tree was whispering something, or singing. If so, it was a lament – a song about someone too beautiful to be happy. Was it about the boy, or about me?

'Just tune it out, dear,' Grandmother Mermaid advised. 'Tend your garden, and take care of yourself.' That's what she did. Bright and early every morning she would dress herself, with a dozen oysters to adorn her tail, not one less, not even for a day. That was to show how exalted she was. In that mermaid world, only the queen could wear twelve oysters; lesser aristocrats could wear six at the very most. Those were the sumptuary rules.

Grandmother Mermaid advised me not to linger too long when I went onshore to roll around on the beach. I might be seen by a 'tail-mad' human walking around on what she always described as 'two awkward stumps'. Not to mention that I might expose my sensitive skin and scales to too much sun. There were stories about mermaids whose tails had turned red as dulse, dried out and torn, starting at the crux of the forked caudal fin. Mermaids with such torn tails were stranded, and could never return to Atlantica again.

Such are the tales that elders tell young mermaids so they will know not to cross the line or break the rules.

I decided to retell Grandmother Mermaid's tales, and end them in my own way. Lying on the beach, I sat up and propped myself on the two awkward stumps that my dried-out tail had torn into. I stuck them into the sand, as far apart as I could, digging them deeper, deeper, until they were solid enough to support my torso, like the pilings of a foundation. I knew that if I went far enough, and stretched hard enough, and long enough, and with enough conviction and dedication, those stumps would take root and come to life.

6

EVEN MERMAIDS GET THE BLUES

The first time I saw Joanna Leunis's dance, I had a hot flush and tears flooded my eyes. Before then I'd thought I was the only mermaid who'd ever gone to live in the city. When I saw Joanna, I knew she was a former mermaid, the same as me. Her sun-bleached hair was a telltale sign. She was the kind of ex-mermaid I wanted to be, with a strong body that didn't detract in the least from her femininity. I couldn't help it; I reached out towards the screen wanting to touch her closely cropped hair and her strong limbs.

She danced like a mermaid that had metamorphosed into a gorgeous and haughty seabird. Her chest was full, like a drum. She stepped so haughtily, and exquisitely. She was eager to show off her finery, but she was also full of curiosity for the colourful panorama of the world. Everything was new to her. She took one step, then another.

'She's so great,' I told Donny the next time I saw him. 'Someday she's going to be the world champion.'

He watched the video and was non-committal, as usual. 'Too early to say.'

He reminded me that Carmen had sat on the throne at Blackpool for a number of years. Carmen was the queen. Before her, ballroom-dancing queens wore their long hair in a bun, but she cut her black hair short, into a bob with a heavy fringe. She didn't wear many hair clips or other head ornaments. Later on many dancers dyed their hair black and had it styled like the empress of Egypt, hoping to become her.

It wasn't that easy, because of the distinctive way she danced. Her predecessors had danced prettily, even floridly.

'Carmen's a queen,' Donny said. 'She doesn't embellish much. Because she doesn't need to. And take a look at Leunis's centre of gravity. She's too high. It's the influence of ballet or modern dance, maybe jazz. She doesn't look like a traditional ballroom dancer. You know how hidebound the judges at Blackpool can be? If she wants to win, she'll have to start by going a bit lower. She has to lose the influences she's picked up from those other styles of dance.'

I liked her dance for reasons that to Donny were shortcomings, reasons why she still had a long way to go.

It wasn't just her stylistic eclecticism that attracted me, though; it was also that she was preternaturally theatrical. In just a few short minutes she could tell a story, full of striking description and plaintive emotion.

One time, in the three short minutes of a rumba, Joanna strolled languorously out to meet her lover for a promenade down the Champs-Élysées. A breeze caressed her cheek, and the leaves the plane trees had scattered on the pavements crackled under her feet. It must have been early autumn. She felt no regret that summer had passed, only an indescribable sweetness.

Carmen was a sublime dancer, with an incredible body and extremely intense emotions, but she wasn't a raconteur like Joanna. Joanna's choreography was so fine that there was a story in each fingertip.

'Even if she is as amazing as you say,' Donny countered, 'the things you're talking about aren't what the judges want to see. If she wants to win, she'll have to make adjustments.'

Joanna was a special case in ballroom. She was educated, with the air of an intellectual. She was a strident feminist. Yet in her body language, the look in her eye and her tone of voice, she had the allure of a movie star in a musical from the golden age of Hollywood.

She'd been a sickly child, so much so that she'd had to stay off school for a while. She did a lot of reading. Her mother had left her to her own devices, apart from signing her up for dance lessons for her health. Joanna had taken to it like a fish to water, or a bird to air. It was just as Donny said: some dancers are made, others are born. Joanna was someone who turned in circles naturally.

It didn't go well for her when she debuted as a ballroom dancer, because she couldn't find the right partner. It wasn't that nobody wanted to dance with her – quite the contrary. A lot of big names had tried to team up with her, but after six months or a year they'd split up, because all those famous male dancers had to have the upper hand, to be in charge of the choreography and the training, the style and aesthetics. Even the costumes and the hairstyles. They wanted to master her, and she wouldn't let them.

Several match-ups looked smooth on stage, but after the bow they would ignore one another, sometimes for good.

Who would she dance with next? When she partnered with a Polish man called Michael Malitowski, everyone who had been following the saga thought she had had no choice but to lower her standards, because he was average at best. But it turned out to be a partnership of genius.

At first the gap in ability was all too obvious, but as the Confucians say, if your partner is strong, you'll come along. That was, after all, one of the reasons I had wanted to dance with Youlin.

Malitowski went from being of a much lower standard to being able to hold his own, expressing his masculinity without stealing the spotlight from Joanna. He became a stable supporter, his arms a loyal branch on which she could bloom, or a whale on which she could ride through wind and wave.

They made a big splash. Pretty soon they had won all the major competitions in America and Europe, except for Blackpool. At the year's most important event, they were the perennial runners-up. Finally, in 2007, Carmen and her partner Bryan Watson announced their retirement, and the next year Joanna and Michael won.

But Donny was right – I could tell Joanna had compromised. She'd lowered her centre of gravity and except for a certain showy quality she'd reduced the influence of other styles. She took the traditional approach the grand old men and women of ballroom expected, and they rewarded her with fame and fortune. The men who fought with her, and were ranked higher than her, back in the day, had been left far behind.

Before Joanna Leunis, I'd been a fan of another mermaid – another woman dancer who refused to play a submissive role, Viktoria Franova. When Joanna Leunis became champion, just like I said she would, I had enough faith in my judgement to point out Viktoria's good points to Donny.

Donny scoffed, and shook his head. According to him, she wasn't even in the top ten; seventh or eighth at best. She wasn't Joanna, not by a long shot.

'You've got to see her rumba,' I said. I was sure she'd nailed the mood of a woman in love.

This time he ignored me.

A week later, in individual class, he cleared his throat and said: 'I watched some of Viktoria's videos again, and you're right, she's pretty good, but that's it. Including her rumba.'

'I still think you're underestimating her,' I said. 'Anyone can tell who the champion or runner-up is. Beyond that you really have to know what to look for. I know what to look for.

'I've got high hopes for Riccardo Cocchi, too,' I continued. 'He got engaged to his partner, Joanne Wilkinson, who used to be his teacher. They're going to take the championship one of these years. You just wait and see.'

'Don't wait for them, they've broken up already – he dumped her. I don't know who he's with now. It'll be a while before he finds a steady partner.'

Donny returned to Viktoria. 'But she ain't no Joanna, that's for sure. That's about it for her dance career.'

'How do you know?'

'She's been with the same guy, Klaus Kongsdal, for a decade now. He's obviously not as good as she is. He hasn't improved at all, but she's too loyal to switch. She isn't going anywhere. She should probably retire. So should he.'

One day Donny announced that he'd found a new partner. She'd practise with him after our individual practice that afternoon.

She made her entrance while I was putting my things in my backpack.

What a coincidence! It was the girl I'd seen smiling in the crowd at the competition, the one who had painted her eyes like Elizabeth Taylor in *Cleopatra*.

Donny introduced her as Mitsuki.

He'd had too many partners in the past year. Who knew how long Mitsuki would last? I could tell he wasn't committed yet, because he treated her with less than the utter devotion he'd shown Susan.

She was actually quite similar to Susan in a lot of ways. They were both muscular yet supple, beautiful and talented. When I got to know Mitsuki better, I gathered that she was also like Susan in her lack of ambition. I never saw her so anxious about a competition that she couldn't eat, or heard her vow to be the champion. Maybe that was why they both got on so well with all the ambitious competitors from our studio, because in their hearts they weren't like that.

Mitsuki didn't want dance to be the centre of her life, but

unlike Susan she went on competing all the same. Now that she was Donny's partner, I went to root for them at competitions. When they got a contract to perform at some corporate event, I tagged along. It was a chance for me to get closer to her.

Whatever Donny's reservations were, I had none. Mitsuki was great to talk to, about *The Avengers*, the curative properties of turmeric, best practices for hair-curling, the invention of International Klein Blue, Prince William's eyes and what colour blue they were. 'One could get lost in those eyes,' Mitsuki said dreamily, like an incurable romantic. But when our conversations got a bit more personal, I realised that she'd been hurt before, and that there was a note of sorrow in the sun. In retrospect I realise that I shouldn't have been so surprised, because I knew as well as anyone that even mermaids get the blues.

One night, when Mitsuki came over to my flat for a pyjama party, she told me about an ex-boyfriend, her first love. She was at college when she'd fallen in love with him, and he was twenty-eight. To me now, even twenty-eight is young, and college students are kids. Anyway, he was half a dozen years older than her. He was treating her more and more strangely, but she couldn't work out if he was angry about something or just wanted to call it a day. He had an acid tongue and kept using it to insinuate that she wanted to go out with other men. She was too casual. Or loose. Yes, sometimes he could be really hurtful in his choice of words. He would also flinch when she tried to touch him, giving her a nasty look, or a look of disgust. He would push her down and twist her arm behind her back, like a cop subduing a suspect in a film. He twisted it until she cried out in pain.

She tried to understand what he was thinking and feeling. He must have been jealous, she thought, of all the men he imagined wanted to go out with her. That must have meant he loved her. He was scared of losing her but felt unable to get her to stay. And so he got angry, and couldn't help hurting the one he cared about the most. It was just a passing phase and couldn't be helped.

The phase didn't pass. He kept being abusive to her, but occasionally showing her some concern. Or so she thought. 'How have you been feeling lately? Are you OK?' Stuff like that.

'I'm fine, thanks. Do I not look well?' she answered.

Several days later he asked again. She said she was fine. But then he asked a third time. Now she was suspicious, but she gave the same answer. This time he pushed her and yelled at her.

'You filthy slut – who knows who you've been carrying on with behind my back?'

He was so mean, and there was so much hate in his

voice. She didn't deserve it, of course, but she swallowed her pride. She thought she'd better make sure there hadn't been some misunderstanding.

She looked him in the eyes. 'There's only you, there's only ever been you. Why would you say that?'

'Who knows?' he said, snickering.

She started crying. He was being a bully. Maybe he was a bully, but she had to give him the benefit of the doubt. She loved him, after all. So she reached out to him again.

'You've got the clap, you cunt! Don't you touch me!'

She was stunned. She'd been going to classes, writing her essays, working part-time, waiting for him, spending time with him, spending money on him. When they went out for dinner, she would always pay. When he came over to sleep with her, he'd 'borrow' whatever she had on hand so he could pay his rent or even have enough for his daily expenses. He knew she was well-off, and could rely on her family no matter what. So to him there was nothing wrong with taking her money and letting her treat him, even if it was with money she'd made herself. And now he accused her of infidelity, now he cast aspersions on her health, now he expressed disgust for her.

'No, I don't! What are you talking about? I . . . ' She was too tired to continue.

'Prove it. Do the test.'

'Why would you even think such a thing?'

'See? You don't want to do it. That means you know you're guilty, you just don't want to admit it.' He pushed her again. She stumbled back, but didn't fall. 'Last time we were together, and one time before that, you left a white blob on me. It was huge. It was so gross. What else could it be besides VD?'

Finally she understood. She didn't know whether to laugh or cry. And so she laughed and cried.

What a moron he was! How had she let herself fall in love with this man without checking his IQ and his common sense first? The white blob, which he'd diagnosed based on his knowledge of the popular lexicon of venereal diseases, was what gynaecologists call leucorrhoea and what women everywhere call cheese. She tried to explain this to him. 'Sometimes it's white, like parmesan; some-times it's yellow, like cheddar.'

'You think it's funny?!' He pushed her one last time and left.

She groaned, the way you might if you discovered your life had turned into a farce, and that only you were to blame.

So what did she do? The next time she met him she took his hand, which he slapped away. She swallowed her pride one more time, and tried to give him a lesson in basic female physiology. 'It's a vaginal discharge,' she said. 'It's normal; all girls get it from time to time, especially when you wear tight trousers. I guess I should stop doing that. Sometimes it leaves a line on your underwear, which is why we sometimes call it the whitebelt. Sometimes it's runny. Sometimes it's solid, and pieces of it will break off.'

'Discharge my arse. You just think I'm ignorant.'

'Ignorant is exactly what you are,' she yelled, but not out loud. She felt guilty, and that she shouldn't look down on her lover. So, in a tender tone of voice that by this point had become an act, she repeated, 'It's not VD.'

'Come on! You just want to avoid admitting the truth, that you're a dirty slut, or why wouldn't you agree to get tested?'

'I can get tested?' she asked. 'Where? Where can I get this kind of thing tested?'

He stared at her as though he'd got the better of her, like he had won. He pushed her on to his scooter and almost dragged her to the hospital. She went through triage, got a number, sat down and waited, trying to be patient. She would pay, like she always did; that went without saying. But maybe the price he'd pay for this health education class was higher.

The doctor did a pelvic exam, the nurse a blood test. Mitsuki would have to wait a week for the result.

After it was done she sat back down by his side. She was so out of it. 'Aren't you going to get tested yourself?' she asked. 'Seeing as we're at the hospital?'

If it weren't for the doctors and nurses, he would have smacked her, she thought. 'I don't need to!' he hissed, through his teeth. In his understanding, VD was disgusting but not contagious.

He marched out of the hospital without saying goodbye. She trotted behind him. He said he had to go to work, and got on his scooter. Evidently, she was to take the bus.

That was apparently it, the end of the story. She started to play with her loose curls. I was sitting on the ground drinking a Coke. She was drinking a Super Supau, a sports drink. We still had some crisps and pot-stickers – pan-fried dumplings – to eat. Mitsuki wasn't too hungry. She asked me if I had any nail polish in the bathroom. I got out a bottle of poppy red and asked if it would do. Of course it would, she said. She started doing her toenails. I threw her a little stool to rest her foot on so it would be easier to apply. She looked content. Mitsuki had deep-set eyes like a westerner. Each eye was a deep pool.

'I'll tell you a story about discharge,' I said. 'It's about my mum. You'd think, being a woman, that she would have known better. Before I knew anything about what goes on between a man and a woman, my mother was really strict. She tried to keep me hermetically sealed. Like when I expressed enthusiasm for an after-school art class that happened to be taught by a man, she withdrew me and had me learn ink wash painting with an old lady. We did orchids and plums, bamboos and chrysanthemums – the four "gentlemen" of classical Chinese painting. You never saw four guys with less sex appeal.

'She'd follow me to school. After I got back she'd admonish me for talking to the boy at the next table at the library. When she realised she couldn't keep me under constant surveillance, she thought she'd better just warn me. "Don't let a boy touch you," she said, "especially not down there." There was murder in her voice, but she said it with a smile. Down there? It was only when I got a bit older that I realised what she meant.

'My mother needn't have worried about me. I never let boys touch me, all through secondary school. It wasn't that I didn't want them to – I did. I'd felt waves of hot, burning desire, and I fantasised, like any other girl. But when an actual man touched me with his hands or kissed me on the lips, I would smell the scent of his desire, and fire would turn to ice. I just couldn't get aroused, I couldn't continue.

'I often wondered why she didn't show the same concern about my stomach, my spleen, my colon or my heart. Why didn't she care about these other organs, just my sex organs? It was as if all that was important about my existence was my vagina.

'Come to think of it, she also obsessed over my stomach, and in an equally vindictive way. Feeding me was a waste of her precious time. "Hurry up so I can clean up," she'd say. The slower I ate the more of her time it would waste. Only foolish women let themselves end up in the kitchen, which is the fate into which she'd let herself fall. Food wasn't nourishment; it was poison. It was the means by which I'd poisoned my mother's life. But when my father was around, she was happy to cook his favourite dishes, especially seafood. I could forget about snacks. Every pea cracker was an insult she took personally. No wonder I mostly prefer to eat by myself. It's more relaxing. Although, look at me now! Here I am eating junk food with you. I've come a long way.

'Anyway, in the evening she would go through my garments in the laundry basket, especially my undergarments. For ages, I just assumed that she was sorting the clothes, looking for stains. I thought it must be normal. But when she got to my panties it was like she was asserting sovereignty. They weren't my clothes, because she'd bought them. It wasn't even my body, because she'd had it. Somewhere along the way, my sense of boundaries got muddled, or maybe it had never been established. Of course I can only express myself in such terms now.

'Once, my mother called me over. She took my dirty underwear out of the basket and interrogated me: "What's this?" she demanded. "What's what?" I asked sheepishly. "This?" She was staring at me. I saw, a sticky white clump of you know what, a sizeable one. I often got them. Why would she get angry about it today? "It's cheese. What else could it be?" I said. "It's a cum stain!" she yelled. "No, it's not!" By that point I could have answered that I was a virgin, but I knew I had better shut up. Maybe I had already said too much.'

Mitsuki didn't say anything or respond in any way. I sat there with a silly smile on my face, then I laughed out loud. I laughed so hard that my stomach hurt. It was getting kind of awkward. Finally, Mitsuki started laughing, too. She collapsed in a heap on top of me.

'So tell me,' I said. 'What did the results from the test say?'

'Leucorrhoea. "Keep your little sister dry," the nurse said. "Don't let it get stuffy down there. Of course it isn't VD, don't be silly."'

'What did the guy say?'

'He read the report but he didn't say anything.'

'He knew how to read?' I couldn't help it.

"'Course he knew how to read. He finished school, you know.'

'My mum took advanced anatomy at university. She knew the human body inside out, a lot better than I did. But when it came to me, she didn't use her knowledge, or common sense.'

'The guy who said I had VD told me his wife would do the same thing. Check his underwear, the pair he'd changed out of the night before, every morning, right in front of him. Like she was asserting sovereignty, was I think how you put it.'

'He had a wife?'

'At the time he did. I don't know about now.'

Well then. That must have been the end of it.

'What do you think the best part about ballroom is?' Mitsuki asked.

'You get to hold someone, rub against each other, and twist back and forth?' I said, foaming at the mouth. 'And pose like a diva?'

I was brushing my teeth.

'It's the costumes,' Mitsuki said. That was her answer.

'What?'

'The costumes. I dance ballroom for the costumes. All that glitter, and the tassels and embroidery. The rhinestones and hairclips ... When you start swinging, under the sparkling light of the mirror ball, you're like a glimmering sea creature swimming along, skirting the sand. The dance floor is as wide as the sea, and all the sequins on our costumes sparkle like the scales of some exotic fish.'

As expected, I couldn't sleep. I tossed and turned while big-boned Mitsuki slept beside me in my bed, limbs exposed. I turned over and saw her there, all curled up. I eased closer to her.

Perhaps in response to something she was dreaming, she reached towards my tummy. She was taller than me, but with her forehead on her knees and her knees on my abdomen she didn't take up too much space. The top of her head was nestled just below my ribs. Her poppy-red toes were resting on my leg.

I caressed her back, lightly, once, then another time. Like I was comforting a child.

Or like I was pregnant with Mitsuki, rubbing my baby bump.

7

A Necklace of Pearls

In retrospect, the time I spent dancing was the happiest period in my life. I've strung the memories into a necklace of pearls, each one rich in hue and fluid of line. In them I can see reflections of flying hems and flexing muscles. On them I can see the residue of sweat. They are reminders of my desire to improve, the excitement I felt pushing my limits all those years ago.

One time Donny was teaching me the queen of the Latin dances, the rumba. It's the queen because it is the source of the steps for all the other dances. If you dance the rumba right, then you have a foundation to build on; you can go on to the cha-cha, samba, and jive. Competitors will go round the classroom doing 'the rounds', meaning their rumba steps, at least two hundred of them, first thing every class.

Though I'm a meatfoot, I'm really flexible from ballet. Donny didn't know. One day he'd included a sequence that he thought would test my flexibility to the limit. We started out standing side by side. He was looking over his right shoulder at me like I was Aphrodite incarnate, the girl of his dreams, while I was looking coyly away. I shifted my weight towards him and pivoted right, slicing a cone of air with my extended left leg. When I'd made a full orbit I raised my left knee to the level of my navel and extended my lower leg to fulfil the promise of the knee, higher and higher, until Donny called cut.

'That's enough, Summer, your leg's already at a hundred and twenty. I'll stand here.' He put his left shoulder at my right, so that our torsos formed a V. He clasped my left hand in his right and put his left hand around my waist. I put my right arm around his shoulders. 'You'll lean back on me,' he said, 'I'll support you. You'll be able to hold your leg straight up. It's going to look fabulous.' I leaned towards him until my right leg was at a 60-degree angle to the floor, parallel to his left leg, and my left leg was pointed nearly straight up.

I took it from the top to the music, ending with a straight leg at 120 degrees to the floor. I gazed into the mirror, as if hoping, proudly but longingly, to catch sight of my Romeo.

Donny glowed approval. 'Well done! Wait for me,' he said. But instead of supporting me, he stood facing me. He cupped my calf and gave it a tentative lift. It lifted easily.

I've got an awe-inspiring range of motion. In the end, I was doing the standing splits. My shin was basically at my temple.

'Fantastic, Summer, just like a pro. I'm going to have to rethink the choreography.' He was pleased.

I was pleased, too. I stood there grinning, a human pole, from the ball of my left heel to the tips of my right toes. I breathed into my abdomen, kept my chest high, and smiled as if I were posing for a hundred cameras, a mermaid in the centre of a parquet sea.

'It's that time of month, I see,' he whispered.

'What? How'd you know?' I kept staring in foolish wonder at my proud face atop my beautifully extended body in the mirror.

'Your wings are showing,' he said, pointing it out discreetly.

I looked down. Inside my little black dance dress, I was wearing black panty shorts, over which I'd wrapped the two white flaps. Because the dress and shorts were black, the flaps were even more conspicuous than they would normally have been.

Donny tittered, then laughed out loud.

Still leaning on him, I realised I wasn't a proud, elegant seabird any more. I flushed scarlet, jerked my leg down and rushed away from the mirror, out of the classroom. I locked myself in the bathroom.

I sat on the toilet a long while, peeved and mortified. There was nothing I could do to hide it. I hadn't brought extra pads with me, and those would have been white anyway. It was a long time before I got up the nerve to go out and face the music. I took a deep breath.

Donny was grinning as I walked over. 'Oh, don't be shy!' he said, like a naughty boy.

My face went red all over again. 'Everyone must have seen ... '

'Nobody saw a thing, they were all practising their steps. You know what it's like: you're focused on yourself. Nobody was staring at your groin.'

'Really?'

'You want to keep practising the move we were just doing?' he said, as if he couldn't wait.

'You've got to be kidding!'

But he wasn't, and so we kept going.

Another time I learned a fun elaboration of a feminine affectation. There are a number of such elaborations in ballroom dance, such as caressing your hair or hips, or raising your dress to let the hem fly. It's supposed to look spontaneous, like a sudden upsurge of Eros, but you have to learn it and practise it. It certainly didn't come naturally to me.

We were holding a static pose with our limbs out near

the end of our routine when Donny suddenly ordered a different ending. 'Now run your fingers through your hair, slide your palms down, add a flourish. I'll finish with you.'

I looked at him woodenly.

He looked back at me impatiently. 'Hurry up!' he said.

'I ... I don't know how.'

'Run your hands through your hair, slide them down, twist your hips a bit, finish with your hands up. Do it! Now!'

I was frozen.

He paused the music. 'Come on, Summer, just vogue. What's the big deal?'

'I really don't know how.'

He looked disgusted, the way he always did when he thought a student wasn't trying.

'Please teach me. I really don't know how, but I want to learn.' I was hurt. It wasn't that I wasn't trying.

'What? Women are fiddling with their hair all the time. It's just a more elaborate version of that. How can you not know how?'

'I really don't. Show me, please ... '

He rocked back, cocking his head, narrowing his eyes. He was still dubious. Finally, he relented. He took a deep breath and demonstrated.

As usual, he broke the sequence up into steps, labelling them as he did them one by one. 'Remember to style your fingers – you don't want to look like a stripper! Now touch

your hair and slide your palms over your neck, your chest
and your waist. Then snap your arms straight. Hold them
a bit out and rock your hips. Three a four a ... whip your
hands above your head on the last midbeat of the bar.
Palms up!'

He did the whole sequence to the music. Sinuously.

'When you rock your hips you can lift your skirt, if it's
long enough. Kind of like this.'

I could feel my eyes shining. I was in awe!

Then I faced the mirror and practised the steps until I
could do the whole sequence, slowly at first, but then faster
and smoother. You could really do it in two beats.

Donny nodded. And then he taught me another way
of doing it. It was basically the same, but you crossed one
arm in front of your face, slid your palm down the opposite
cheek, tossed your head and uncrossed your arm as you
slid your palm across your chest. The rest was the same.

'You've got to remember to stay centred when you
rock your hips, with your knees slightly bent, like in the
basic stance.'

I kept practising.

'I'd never have thought,' said Donny, 'that I'd be teaching
a woman how to do a hair flick.'

I shrugged and apologised.

Now I knew.

*

Another time, Donny forbade me from wearing a certain white T-shirt to the group class because it made me look busty. When you're dancing and your boobs are going up and down, it can be really distracting, he told me.

'It's just a white T-shirt. Haven't I been wearing one all along?'

'I don't know why it's different – maybe it's the fabric – but whatever it is, the uncles are staring at your boobs. If the uncles keep doing that, then the aunties will find an excuse to come and teach you a lesson. You'll get ostracised. Do I have to explain everything to you?'

It seemed that Donny had a thing or two to teach me outside of dance that he'd learned from all the women he'd taught or danced with over the years.

Donny and I often watched videos together – not just dance videos, but also music and choreography videos, and videos on new hairstyles and costumes. As we watched we would discuss the many talents an elite competitor had to have beyond dance, especially costume design. No matter what, the costume is supposed to accentuate your waist and your hips, 'because that's where the action is'. Beyond that, if the costume can highlight a competitor's specific physical qualities and dance abilities, or give her a distinctive look, it can be a big advantage. Carmen's dresses were all on the long side. Some had tassels that went past the knees. She represented a traditional sex appeal that didn't flaunt itself. As Donny said, she had the dignity of a queen. Yulia Zagoruychenko, for whom Riccardo Cocchi dumped his former teacher, dressed more like a fashion model than a dancer. She wore supple feminine costumes. She gathered her platinum blonde hair into a big bun, or a vertical ponytail, pulling her skin so taut it looked as if the corners of her eyes were going to shoot off towards her wispy sideburns. Even when she didn't dance particularly well, she was unforgettable, like an actress.

Susan had worn short tube skirts with a lot of tassels, like a North American Indian woman in a film. That was the design for her headwear, too. Mitsuki mostly wore little bubble skirts, but the size and fit was similar, because she and Susan had the same basic body type. As for me? Donny once knelt down and pulled at my Lycra practice skirt until it turned into a tube skirt. 'Look, you've got beautiful legs, but no backside. This kind of tube shape can show off your strengths and hide your pancake butt. If you ever go and compete someday, you can just borrow their costumes.'

Donny not surprisingly had strong opinions about costuming. He hated the vintage women's head ornaments from the jazz age that there had been a vogue for. They were fine for flappers in The Great Gatsby, but not on ballroom dancers' heads. They looked all right to me.

Costumes that spliced in new materials with a stiff texture were another of Donny's pet peeves. 'It doesn't look like a costume,' he complained. Such a costume didn't swing to accentuate a dancer's movements. He preferred the traditional multi-layered gauze skirt with tassels and glitter, which did. But that was the latest fashion, I told him. The magazines had been doing features. The dancer in the photo that offended his sensibilities was obviously trying to marry avant-garde fashion and ballroom. Her efforts deserved to be applauded.

'It's hideous. How could I applaud it? Overall, variations on tradition, but in a traditional context, work best.'

'Because that gives you a better chance at winning?'

'Exactly.'

It had occurred to me that I was only able to get so close to Donny on account of his sexual orientation. Even if he was just teaching me how to dance, I'd have felt a physical refusal, or at least I would have held back, if he had been straight. Sex would have got in the way. I'm not talking about sexual attraction, but rather the reverse: revulsion is a kind of negative attraction. It would have prevented me from becoming such good friends with him. He couldn't have become my teacher.

For a lot of people who are learning partner dance or getting used to a new partner, a faint erotic energy is helpful. It can get things moving along smoothly. Many people find it stimulating, but I didn't. I'd learned that about myself early on. Before Donny, I had a dance teacher who'd graduated from a national university, which for most girls would have been a plus. He also looked studious. He sounded like a bumpkin, but maybe I could have got over my prejudice against people from the countryside. What I couldn't get over was his faintly erotic energy, like a piece of gravel in my shoe. I couldn't open my heart to him. I couldn't learn from him. I was stiff in class, frigid. I felt frustrated, like I was wasting my money, so I quit. It was for the best, because he wasn't really that good.

With Donny, of course, and with Youlin, thank God, I never had the nagging worry that I would become a sex fantasy. I could open my heart and body and take in new things, and I could go places I'd never been to before. Donny could take me to such places, into a bustling, boisterous world of saturated colour and fluid light. He showed me the way to that world. He baptised me, and I dived in at the deep end. Finding myself underwater, I admired all the sights and sounds. Sometimes Donny was there, occasionally Youlin was there, too, swimming beside me, but I could also swim alone; it could be one person's struggle, one person's vision, one person's world. It was just like Donny said: the dance floor was a secret world of solitude, a world to escape into when everything in the real world seemed too much to bear. Humans who've never been to this world will envy those who know it, for the unearthly expressions on their faces.

'When did you know?'

'From the start.'

I didn't imagine many of his students knew, because he was low-key, and because the dance logic of 'men lead, women follow' had been spliced into the fabric of his being.

'How did you find out?'

Donny was a special case. He was a gay gentleman. As a gentleman, he was the good kind of traditional guy. When we went to dinner, he felt it was his duty to treat me and see me home. He would escort me down the street. We'd be walking side by side, and he would put his hand around my shoulders, instinctively protecting me, whether as an extension of the leader's intuitive ability to guide his partner so she wouldn't be jostled by other competitors, or simply because he was concerned about me. But I always knew he could never be attracted to me.

'First time we danced, from the moment you took my hand, I could tell. I'd never had a partner like that before, someone with such powerfully firm hands, who could lead so forcefully and clearly. I felt such a tenderness towards you, like I knew I could rely on you, depend on you utterly. But there was nothing sexual in the signal you sent, in all the good things that attracted me to you, that you conveyed to me through your lead hand. There were a lot of different things, but not an iota of sex. I'd danced with a lot of men, and whether they danced well or poorly, whether they liked me or not, whether they looked down on me or worshipped me, it was the same to me: the foundation was sexual. I could feel it. But with you that was entirely lacking.'

Donny forced a smile.

The rumba, the cha-cha and my favourite, the jive, are supposed to express heterosexual love.

'But that can't be what you feel when you dance. How do you do it?' I asked.

'Haven't you heard of Stanislavski?' he replied. 'When I act the part of a lover, then I'm in love.'

'I see. But there must be limits?'

'Sure there are. The Di Filippo twins, Stefano and Annalisa, danced the jive so fast they were like robots. It was synchronised dancing. It was really impressive. But everyone, the audience and the judges, knew they were brother and sister. How could they possibly act out heterosexual attraction, especially in the rumba? So they plateaued at third or fourth, and couldn't get any higher. They were amazing, and they always got an amazing score, but it was never beautiful, let alone sultry. You wouldn't have wanted it to be.'

'I told you we'll be late for our class. Hurry up. Hey, I've got something here that'll help.' He finished putting on his jeans, got something out of the drawer in the headboard of his bed and tossed it at me. It was a package of sanitary napkins. When I caught it, the bath towel fell. I looked down at the package, then round the room, still dazed. I still wasn't sure what it all meant. I felt something weighing on my solar plexus.

I zoned out again in the bathroom. In the end I ripped open the package and put some other girl's pad on my little sister.

I was quiet for a while.

'Please don't fight, you and Donny.'

Mitsuki just changed the channel.

Donny was torn. Should he keep trying to convince Mitsuki to be more professional or give up and start looking for another partner, again? He was up and down. His students could tell when he wasn't in a good mood.

One night we went for hotpot. He helped me peel the shrimp and cook it, as usual. Some habits were hard to break.

He said he'd come to a realisation. He felt so tired and alone. He should just find a regular partner to keep him company and share his life with. Not a dance partner; someone to live with.

'What kind of partner are you looking for?' I asked.

He answered like a bashful girl, but it wasn't an answer a bashful girl would have given. 'I'm looking for someone with the usual qualities one looks for in a partner: decent appearance, steady income, similar level of education, similar tastes and interests. That's about it.'

'How are you any different from any straight woman you might see walking down the street?'

He seemed not to hear. 'I'm really not that kind of guy,' he said, 'but I've sure dumped my share of girls over the years.'

I gritted my teeth at his word choice.

Smiling, he counted the hearts he'd broken on his fingers. 'What about me? Why don't we get married?'

He looked up and his eyes grew bright and keen. It was a calculating look. I was taken aback. I knew he had been around the block, but he'd never given me a look like this. This was not the Donny I could fool around with, the Donny who had a passion for teaching, no matter how poor the student was, whether in money or ability.

'What's in it for you?' he said.

'What?'

'What would you get out of marrying me?'

'I never thought about it. What I want is a teacher, and a family.'

He chortled. 'I see. I'm your teacher, I could be your

family. But what would you bring to the table? I don't need a teacher.'

I was speechless.

'I forgot to mention that I'm looking for a partner who is a bit younger than me,' he said. 'She should be stable, and agreeable. She'd keep my parents company and hang out with the extended family on occasion. You're not the kind of girl I could bring home, the kind my mother would be satisfied with. You know what I mean.'

Holding my heart in my hands, I said, 'Then how are you any different from a typical straight man you might see walking down the street?'

8

GRAVITY

I don't recall how many times my old landlord appeared
in drag after he came covered in purple bling to buzz me
out of bed. I got used to it – and ready for it. I'd run to the
door as soon as the bell rang and hand over the rent.

He was more flamboyant every time. At first it was
shells. Later it was pearl earrings and gold necklaces. I'd
see him once a month like that in my doorway counting his
money. I was unfazed. It came to seem normal, especially
because I had made friends with another crossdresser, the
teenage son of a professor's widow who lived upstairs, on
the seventh floor.

The son had started by letting his hair grow long and
getting it to stay in place with a hairband. Then he tried
women's lace blouses, which he matched with skinny
jeans. He could get away with it, because he was tall and

thin, and because there's a fine line between transvestite and glam rock star.

He often listened to music with headphones, and one time I smiled at him and asked him what it was – David Bowie? David who? He said he was listening to a Japanese band called Kanjani Eight. Another time I asked him what he was thinking of becoming. He said a comic-book artist. I said great.

One afternoon he came down in the lift wearing black tights, a black leather miniskirt, a thick black leather belt and a sheer, airy white blouse. He'd done his hair and put on makeup. I smiled at him and said hello. 'Please don't tell my mum!' he replied.

'Don't worry!' I said, and shook my head. 'I wouldn't.'

So it went for quite a long time – more than half a year. One night I'd zoned out on the balcony when I saw someone slink out of the alley. I thought it might be my teenage friend, but I wasn't sure. Whoever it was was wearing a goose-yellow nightgown with a thin white collar, and a pair of furry white slippers. Something seemed off, like it was him but something had changed.

You could tell at a glance that my neighbour was a boy in women's clothing, and not just visually. It was a kind of scent. It was a man's smell, even though he was effeminate. But the impression I got from this person was different. It – no, she – was a girl. You could just smell it.

But it's late, I thought, I can't be so sure. I waited there for over ten minutes until the person reappeared in the same outfit, but coming the other way from the other end of the alley. He or she must have walked around the block. Now I could see him or her from the front.

It was him – no, it was her. Something had changed inside. Somehow he'd managed to turn himself into a girl.

I hadn't noticed the landlord's failure to appear, until a pale, fleshy, long-haired woman came to collect the rent. She introduced herself as the landlord's granddaughter. The landlord had passed away the previous week, she said. I should arrange for my account to be debited in future. It was one less thing for everyone to worry about. Who pays the rent in person any more?

'Last week?' I said.

'Yeah, on Tuesday night.'

As she wrote her bank details on a piece of white paper, with her telephone number, I looked her over, to fill in the details of my first impression: fine, narrow eyes, long lashes, a full white face like a steamed dumpling, a well-proportioned nose and mouth. She was younger than I had first thought – in her twenties.

The old fellow and his family lived downstairs. They had a big garden, like the people on the ground floor of a mid-rise in Taiwan often do. Was I awake last Tuesday night? Was I lying in bed, or sitting on the balcony, watching the neighbourhood? If I was awake at that time, did I notice anything other than a stray cat screeching? Maybe the landlord's spirit had passed right by me without my noticing. Would he have stopped and greeted me, maybe to remind me to pay the rent?

I had never noticed who was in his family, or that he even had a granddaughter, let alone what she looked like. But from then on, our paths kept crossing. I'd be carrying home the groceries and she'd be taking her kid out. We'd stand in the doorway and she'd stop to chat, to tell me all about her son or her husband. She really liked her husband. Good for her. No matter how long we talked, from pleasantries to the chat proper, she was sure to mention him. I saw him once: he was thin and dark. I guess opposites attract.

On one occasion, she told me her grandfather had been behaving strangely for a long time before he died. The family didn't know what to do. He had started to behave effeminately. He'd go through the wardrobe and try on his wife's finery. He wore her jewellery, her hairclips, her sunglasses. Sometimes he'd go out in her clothes. It was as if he had mistaken himself for his dead wife, her grandmother.

But sometimes he was a different person entirely. One time he snuck up on his daughter-in-law, her mother, in the kitchen and tried to force himself on her from behind. The daughter-in-law screamed and tried to shake him off. His son had to rush over to tear them apart. The son called his father a senile old lech.

'She's my wife!' his father had yelled back. 'Why can't I?' Then he was sobbing. 'You pick on me, yell at me. You won't let me see my own wife.'

Sometimes he thought he was his dead wife, sometimes he mistook his daughter-in-law for her.

'For a while my mum was too scared to come home.'

Meixin and her fiancé were still taking an individual class with Donny. It was right before mine. So we'd see each other four times a week, twice in group class, twice in the studio. In the studio, every time, she'd come and sit by me and say a few words. Sometimes she'd share personal stuff with me, which I wasn't expecting. I thought we were still just acquaintances. I imagined something must have been weighing on her mind or she wouldn't have unburdened herself.

In theory, they'd been in a competition, so Donny hoped they'd keep refining their craft. Meixin wanted to. But her fiancé suddenly started missing the individual classes. When I got there I'd often see Meixin and Donny practising. Sometimes Meixin would just skip the class to avoid Donny's questions.

I only heard the marriage was off a few months later.

The aunties and uncles were surprised. They looked so much alike, they had the face of a married couple. And both of them were computer engineers. They'd been engaged for six years. How could it be off?

Meixin lost her companion in life, and her dance partner.

She couldn't get over it. She was listless in the aunties and uncles class, partly because of their solicitous looks and, because she didn't have a partner, she had to dance with air. She'd never done it before, and couldn't get used to it.

'You're so lucky to have Youlin,' she said.

Meixin's parents had divorced when she was young. Her mother had raised her. According to her, her father was irresponsible, though she didn't say in what respect. I'd heard that before. Every classmate whose parents were divorced would deliver the same line, that Mum or Dad was irresponsible. It depended on who they'd ended up with.

Meixin said she was lucky to have her mother. But her mother didn't like Meixin's fiancé. It had been such a long time, but the mother wasn't intending to let them get married any time soon. She was always pointing out his flaws.

On one occasion, the studio had rented a hall to put on another event. This one was in-house, not a formal competition. There were performances by some of the studio competitors, and even one by the founder and his wife. It was a chance for the newer students to get some experience performing in front of an audience and for the rich lady students to spend a fortune on a bespoke costume or two.

The founder invited everyone to bring their families to take part in the fun. After all, many of the students relied on their parents to pay the tuition. Meixin brought along her mother and aunt. Her fiancé brought his parents along with a paternal uncle and a few cousins. It was a chance for the two families to get to know one another. It hadn't gone well.

'My aunt claims my fiancé's uncle tried to cop a feel on the dance floor. My mum made a scene. The uncle insisted he hadn't tried to cop anything, and the fiancé's family was flustered. After it was all over my mother went over to give them another piece of her mind. By then they had hardened their hearts.'

Meixin and her boyfriend had drifted apart and split up.

Meixin kept following his Facebook after the break-up, and realised he'd got over her a lot quicker than she'd got over him. He was going out with someone at work. He'd started dancing because of Meixin. And now he didn't have to dance any more. Her conclusion was that he'd fallen in love with someone else in just half a year, so obviously her mother had been right all along. Her mother had more experience, and better judgement, than she did when it came to men.

Meixin decided to take the ballroom class Donny's

teacher, the founder of the studio, put on for college students. Maybe she would be able to find a partner in the class, someone young like Youlin. The founder took special care of girls without partners by dancing with them and looking out for potential partners for them.

Eventually he set her up with a studio competitor nicknamed Chubby. He could just as well have been called Shorty. As you can imagine, he stood out among all the lean, muscular dancers. He'd tried a lot of partners, but no one was a good fit. He had some experience, but that kind of physique wouldn't work to his advantage at a competition, to say nothing of his middling technique. He'd started at the studio a few years after Donny, but had never caught up, or even come close. He wasn't getting any better.

In the past he'd been berated by partners who were better than him. Now he had the chance to berate Meixin. She wasn't a competitor, and wasn't that experienced. She hadn't practised for a while. Chubby felt superior. He would correct the smallest mistake. It was a change of perspective for Meixin, too. When she'd danced with her former fiancé, she was the one who did the correcting.

It hurt her feelings, and sapped her confidence. But she wanted a partner, and Chubby was a competitor. With him she had a chance to be a competitor, too. She tried harder.

As for me, even though Youlin hadn't officially acknowledged me as his partner, we had danced together for such a long time that it felt like it could be left unsaid. In group class he would walk by my side, as if he saw me as his partner. The aunties and uncles certainly saw us as a pair. When he came in late the uncles would tell me, 'Summer, go and dance with the young pup.'

For a while at least I had the consolation that I belonged to someone, and that someone belonged to me. I had a dancer's sense of security. I'd formed a pair with a fellow human.

When Youlin's dad invited me out for another dance with them, I was tempted to politely decline. I felt I'd already passed the test. But we were a steady pair now, and they meant well, so I went anyway. The five of us went out together to have some fun. This time we went to a salsa club a lot closer to my house in the east end in the evening. It would be a younger crowd.

Everyone was smiling, Youlin seemed happy.

We went in and squeezed through a writhing mass of young people twisting their hips under the strobe lights until we found a table along the wall. Youlin's parents disappeared into the crowd. Youlin's smile was gone, too. He appeared to be pouting – who knows what about? He wasn't talking. I wondered if I'd done something to offend him. His brother sat down and tried to defuse the tension. That was a relief. But then his phone vibrated and he said he had to go out. He winked at me before he did. 'I really don't like dancing, or I'd ask you to salsa.'

Youlin still wasn't talking to me or looking at me. When I tried to talk to him he pretended not to hear. After a while he just walked off, leaving me there alone.

I tried to keep smiling. Youlin's elder brother came back to find me sitting by myself. He smiled knowingly. 'You all right? I'll wait with you.'

I thanked him for being so considerate. Then Youlin reappeared.

'Let's dance,' he said.

'All right,' I said, relieved that he was the one to break the ice.

'Let's dance the routine Donny's been teaching us this month.'

My eyes widened. This was a crowded salsa club; everyone was rubbing up against everyone else. This was no place for the showy throws that Donny had gone to so much trouble to add to our routine. Basically, the man tossed his partner around a lot, which required a lot of space. It was highly dramatic, the kind of choreography you'd see in a competition or a performance. It was really out there. It would be outré in here.

'No, it's too crowded, and it's a salsa club.'

'What are you worried about? I can lead you. A male dancer is supposed to protect his partner – you don't think I can? I can make space, it's not a problem!'

I shook my head. 'Salsa, please.'

It'd be impolite for us to force our way through a crowd of hot, happy kids. But it wasn't just the space; the music wasn't appropriate for rumba, either.

Youlin gave me the silent treatment again, and a nasty look.

But he didn't last a minute before he needed to start nagging me again. 'Come on!'

I insisted, 'Salsa?'

He insisted, 'Rumba.'

I shook my head and looked away. Now it was my turn to refuse to look at him. He sat by my side waiting for me, assuming I'd give in to him like I usually did. When he realised I wouldn't he left in a huff.

I took a deep breath, not knowing whether to laugh or cry. I stood up, intending to visit the ladies' room. But as I did a bald guy happened to be passing by. He pulled me into his arms. He was all sweaty, but dressed fashionably. He was a dandy nightclub hoofer who'd been hotfooting it with a lot of different girls all night. 'I'm going to take you dancing!' I didn't have time to reply, only to acquiesce as he pulled me along, with the hand that had taken mine and the hand that he had put around my waist. Before I knew it, he was leading me, forwards and backwards, round and round. I had had enough after one dance, but he said not so fast, and so we danced one song after another, like maniacs. I let myself get carried away by the wild tempo, the ridiculous rhythm. I was grinning despite myself, and laughed out loud. After I don't know how many numbers, he finally called an end to it, bowed to me like a gentleman and led me back to my seat.

Youlin's brother was still there, smiling. 'I saw you dancing. You looked really happy. It's so great that you were able to have a good time after all.'

I picked up the glass and was quenching my thirst when Youlin appeared again. He slammed down his glass and stared at me.

His elder brother and I were startled.

He pointed at me and yelled: 'Who the hell do you think you are? You refuse to dance with your partner and then you go and have the greatest time with some random bald guy. You're a bitch!'

What a jerk! The kind of hotshot he wanted to be treats a woman right, even if he does so with affected chivalry. But a hotshot's rude aggression, well, it came to him naturally.

He kept yelling, but I'd had enough. I stared back at him, waiting for him to finish his tantrum.

Youlin's elder brother finally got hold of himself and reached out to take his little brother's arm. Youlin pushed his hand away, turned and left.

Youlin's brother forced a smile, shaking his head. He

raised an eyebrow to ask if I was all right. I nodded. We sat there shoulder to shoulder in silence for a few minutes.

'Hey, why don't I take you dancing? Let's have some fun.'

I shook my head and said I'd had enough, I was tired.

I suddenly felt like crying, again. I felt terribly mistreated. I'd had enough of Youlin's abuse. I stood up and told his brother I wanted to go home.

'Are you sure?' he asked. 'Let me see you out.'

'Please don't,' I said. 'I'm fine.'

I started crying in the taxi. What the hell! A young man I barely knew had hurled abuse at me in a public place, for no reason. He slammed his glass on the table for no reason. It was all incomprehensible. It was so unfair, especially as the finale to a year of him rolling his eyes at me, putting me down, coming late, not coming at all, yelling at me at the drop of a hat, blaming me for his own mistakes. How could I have let myself be humiliated by a little man that I wasn't even friends with?

After I got home, I realised that Youlin wanted to be seen by all the dancers who were salsa-ing for all they were worth but might not have his technique. He wanted to be the centre of attention, by dancing the rumba routine his teacher had choreographed for us. I'd worried it would be impolite. There wasn't enough space and we literally wouldn't have fitted in. He didn't want to fit in, to lose himself in the crowd; he wanted to stand out. He wanted everyone to see how tall and handsome he was, how cool he was, how unique. In his fantasy, everyone would watch him do all those difficult moves, in awe of what a great dancer he was. And the audience he cared about most of all was his parents. He wanted his parents to see how good he was – how much better he was than his elder brother. By refusing him, I had denied him his chance to prove himself in his parents' eyes. He wanted it so much, but he couldn't do it alone; he needed me to co-operate. When I wouldn't, he lost it.

I concluded that I'd brought it on myself. I'd invited it, and I'd let myself be humiliated because I was too greedy. I wanted to do partner dance so much that I'd practically pleaded with Youlin to dance with me. I'd lain down and let him walk all over me, and when he did I didn't dare resist, because I was afraid he'd run off. It was because I wanted to dance this kind of dance so so so much – this gorgeous dance of couples who appeared to be joined at the hip.

Actually, I'd been alone, all this time, for as long as I could remember. I just couldn't do it. I'd never been able to enter the world of two make a pair. I'd never really got in the door. I'd begged, I'd pestered, I'd brought it all on myself, because I'd never been willing to face the truth that I'd always been alone and that it bothered me.

The rules were the rules. I'd agreed to play by them, and they had locked me out.

But it was still my fault. If I hadn't been so desperate, if I hadn't left myself so wide open, then nobody in the world could have pushed me around.

There's one thing that is more important in partner dance than anything else. From the basic steps to the most virtuosic flourish, the main thing is that the bodies of the dancers must twine round each other during the dance, or to press so closely together that it seems like they are leaning on one another, when in fact both partners are supporting themselves separately.

If the partners weren't independently rooted, as it were, then none of those amazing flowers could bloom – the flowers a pair can trace as they turn round the dance floor. Some people dance for years without realising this basic truth. They don't understand that what they have to practise every day, over and over, is finding their centre of gravity, their source of stability, and then channelling energy by turning around the axis that goes through the centre of it. If you haven't found it, you can't be stable standing there, let alone channel energy properly when you move. You'll end up pulling on your partner. If you're a man, you can never reliably signal the next step the girl is to perform. If you're a woman, you're unable to translate that signal into stylish motion. Some fools assume that the man is supposed to help the woman turn, by pushing and pulling her, but any such attempt is an external force that might tilt her off balance. She could have kept turning effortlessly, like a top, but instead she topples over.

The leader activates the follower, but the follower has to stay on her toes, waiting for the signal, which she has to translate into movement on her own. He can't help you turn, girls, you have to turn yourself.

So the lead–follow relationship in dance isn't the same as ordinary interpersonal relationships where what looks like intimacy is actually dependency or clinging – holding the other back, tripping the other up or rubbing the other the wrong way.

I once danced with a newcomer in the aunties and uncles class. I was about to turn a 360 when he pushed me.

I stopped dead in my tracks and showed him some eye-ball. 'Why did you push me?'

'I didn't push you,' he retorted. 'I was helping you turn. Isn't that my job – to lead?'

'I don't want your help! Your hand sends me a turn signal, but I will turn on my own. Leading doesn't mean you help me turn.'

Another time I asked Donny about one of the girls in the studio. She obviously knew the steps, but was just as obviously limp, and that makes all the difference to the energy and the quality of the dance. Donny patted my head. 'Most people can't tell.'

In dance it's irresponsible for the follower not to practise finding her own centre of gravity. A follower's dependency is a fatal flaw that will distort the form and skew the lines. Dependency is not in the basic spirit of partner dance, and can never be beautiful. No matter how intimate a pair may seem, how sexy their partnership, each has to stand firm on his or her own two feet. If you're the girl, you wait expectantly. You stay on your toes, so to speak. It may look as if he's supporting and you're leaning. But actually he has to stand firm in his centre of gravity, and so do you. Only then can you co-operate to do the difficult moves. Only then can you maintain a fluid line.

To keep your balance, no matter what move you're doing, no matter what pose you're holding, you have to train yourself daily. There's no way around it. There's no immediate benefit, and only cognoscenti ever see a difference, in the subtle firming of one's core, the supple tautness of one's muscle fibres, and in the flexibility that enhances strength. When you have it, your legs are straight, your chest open, the nape of your neck uplifted. It's the kind of practice that you often overlook because you think you've mastered it already. Fools will say they want to focus on the flowery moves. The wise know to pay constant attention to their centre of gravity.

After Youlin was out of the picture, that's all I was able to do.

Leaves budded only to fall. I kept wearing my skimpy dance skirt, but with a sweatshirt over it to stave off the cold.

Meixin had been trying to dance with Chubby for a year, but Chubby told her she wasn't getting any better, in fact she was even getting worse. She got yelled at so much that she gave up. After hearing how worthless she was, how was she supposed to take his hand and hold him when the music started, to dance the dance of new love? It was too painful.

Donny said pros could do it. A lot of pro competitors looked at each other lovingly on the dance floor, but not off, because they loathed each other.

Meixin got engaged again, to another engineer. Her mother approved and gave her blessing but, just as with the previous one, she started to nit-pick after the engagement. She found all sorts of shortcomings. Getting together was easy; staying together would be hard.

Meixin cancelled her individual class with Donny, and got so frustrated that she split with Chubby. She stopped going to the founder's class, or even to the aunties and uncles class. She gave Mrs Lai a call from time to time to ask if there were any new dancers. If anyone joined who might be a good match for her, she would give it a try.

Youlin quit coming for almost two months after getting

into college. The uncles and aunties were asking me where he was, why he hadn't come now that he'd passed his entrance exams. He was on holiday! He had nothing else to do – he should come. Even Donny asked me to give him a call, because if I didn't, Youlin's father would give him a call sooner or later. I said I didn't know. I really didn't. He didn't take my calls. I didn't want to keep calling.

After that episode in the salsa club, Youlin had kept coming late or missing classes. That didn't surprise me, especially since he had entrance exams to study for. But, one time, when class was half over, who should appear but Youlin? He walked over to me. We were learning a new move: the girl stands with her left hand on her waist and her right hand reaching up, while the boy kneels on one knee and reaches out like Romeo for a tender embrace, with adoration in his eyes.

Everyone was holding the pose, waiting for Donny to adjust their postures, waiting for the next instruction. Amazingly, Youlin knelt down like the other men and looked up at me. I was still angry at him, and not just because of the salsa club incident. I didn't talk to him. I didn't even look at him. I looked ahead to see what Donny was showing us.

Because my right hand was upraised, part of my tummy showed between my T-shirt and my tube skirt. Still kneeling there, Youlin tugged my T-shirt down so it covered my tummy, looking up to see what my reaction would be, like he was trying to make up with me.

I couldn't help it, I felt relieved somehow. In partner dance two strangers press their bodies more intimately than is normal in society. Youlin and I understood each other's bodies much better than we understood each other's hearts. But maybe when you're familiar with the person's body, you'll feel something for them, something like compassion or duty.

Next time he came, he was a college student. As usual, he was an hour and a half late. I was used to it, to practising the new steps in front of the mirror with air in my embrace. What a relief, I thought, now I could really practise. But he hadn't come alone. He'd brought a girl with him, a classmate. He didn't come to stand by me; he sat and chatted with her at the back. Donny and the aunties and uncles looked on, confused and concerned.

During the break, he came over to announce to me that the girl would be his new partner. He was hoping that, since she was learning from scratch, I could show her the ropes.

I was taken aback. 'You want me to show her the ropes?'

'Yeah, like it's break time now, you can teach her something. You're a girl, you're more familiar with the steps. Please. If you don't teach her, I won't be able to dance with her.'

I just looked away. The break was over. 'Positions!' Donny said.

Youlin still wouldn't take no for an answer. 'Come on, Summer. She's waiting.'

'I've paid my tuition, please don't waste my tuition or my time.'

I looked towards Donny, ignoring my former partner. Everyone was staring. Youlin walked indignantly to the back of the classroom and sat down by the new girl's side. They weren't sitting there for long.

After class the aunties and uncles all came over, asking, who does he think he is, coming with a girl during the last break and then leaving? What did he say? I shook my head and smiled wryly. I didn't want to say anything, it was too embarrassing.

I filled Donny in on the details during individual class the following weekend.

'What a spoiled brat!' he said. What else could he say? It was the way of the world.

In the end the pairs split up one by one. Meixin and Chubby. Me and Youlin. Donny and Mitsuki were history, too. But we were all still swimming by ourselves in the ocean, chasing the colours and the currents, dreaming of who we might meet next. If winter comes, can spring be far behind?

*

I actually held out for quite a while, alone in group class.

One night, Donny was teaching us the cha-cha. There were a lot of rapid turns. He wanted us to do a pirouette in a single beat, stopping on the beat, like a ballerina. The smoother and faster your turn, the easier it is to end up facing the same direction.

During break time we kept practising the turns, me in my high-heeled shoes. I turned and turned.

My feet hurt so I took my heels off and stretched my toes. When I felt better I stood up again and did another pirouette.

I straightened my back, lifted my head, opened my chest, breathed into my abdomen, extended my arms, tucked my bum, stood en pointe and swooshed to the right. I'd done everything right, except finding my centre of gravity. I tilted over. I tried to steady myself with my right foot, but instead of the ground I ended up stepping on one of my left toes. And when you're turning fast, you're generating a lot of force. I came down hard. There was an audible crack, followed by a shooting pain. Leaning against the wall, I discovered that the second toe on my left foot was off centre, at a 45-degree angle.

An off-kilter toe – how ugly, I thought. I couldn't stand the sight of it, so I bent down and cracked it back into place.

I decided to pretend it hadn't happened. I figured that by the time I got home I'd have forgotten all about it.

At this time I was seeing a guy named David. He'd come and pick me up after class. I must have mentioned my toe to him, or maybe I was limping. However he found out, he was concerned. Shouldn't he take me to A&E? I told him I'd managed to yank it back into place. I didn't want to go to hospital, I wanted to go on a date with him. I'd be fine.

I was wrong. On the third day it started to swell up, and to turn black and blue. I could only wear sandals and had to use a cane. The day after that I went to see an orthopaedic doctor at a local clinic.

He took an X-ray and told me I'd broken it.

He asked me how it had happened. I tried to explain how and why I had come to crank my misaligned toe back into position. I offered to demonstrate but he shook his head.

'You may have saved yourself without realising it,' he said. If I'd left it askew like that for three days, it might have been gangrenous by now for lack of blood. Then I would have lost it. I'd cracked it in the first place, but by yanking it back I'd made a clean break, which actually allowed for increased blood flow. That was why it took three days before it swelled up so much that I needed to see a doctor.

He put it in a cast and told me not to worry: the swelling would subside and the bone would knit.

'When?' I asked.

'About six months,' he said.

'Six months? Can I keep dancing?'

He laughed out loud. 'How are you going to dance with a broken toe?'

'See you in half a year!' said Donny.

That ended up being a bit of an underestimate. It would be about ten years before I set foot in a dance classroom again.

9

A SECRET WORLD

My boyfriend David likes to take care of his fish. You could call him a hobbyist but it's more than a hobby; it's more like a spiritual pursuit. His big saltwater aquarium is a 'microcosm', he says, like having a miniature sea in his living room. He can watch his fish through the glass, discerning their movements and their moods for hours on end. It gives him a sense of security. At some point, as he gazes out into his sea, he loses himself in the boundless expanse he can imagine the back of the tank opening out into. Then the feeling is more like serenity.

Like Donny, David has a secret world he can disappear into at any time, which belongs to him alone.

David's read up on the history of the aquarium. He's told me all about it. It's of European origin, and can be traced back to the 'cabinet of curiosities' in the early Renaissance.

People collected rare or precious objects and arranged them artfully in glass cases in their homes. The truly rich could devote an entire room to the treasures in their collections.

What did people put in their cabinets early on? Crocodile specimens, or fossilised eggs or plants. Such things were so valuable that they became tokens of the rarefied social circles you had to move in to be able to afford them. To a collector, they also signified another kind of distinction, as if simply by collecting you were an explorer at heart, driven onwards by a burgeoning desire for knowledge of the unknown.

Explorers started to satisfy their desire for knowledge of the unknown, and the vanity of collectors, in the fifteenth century, at the beginning of the age of discovery. They explored the unknown parts of the world, the unlabelled, unmapped gores into which early cartographers divided their globes. The further they ventured, the more rarities from distant seas and shores appeared in the cabinets of curiosities; shells and seahorses were all the rage.

To put these things in the cases, collectors preserved them, catalogued them, classified them and recorded them. Doing so turned collectors into scientists, even educators. There was a fad for sumptuous volumes that summarised the contents of the sea in sets of some four or five hundred cards. Some of the sets were beautiful copperplate prints.

Such a set was supposed to concentrate and represent the entire ocean, like an illustrated encyclopaedia – another kind of microcosm.

The scientists who turned their cabinets of curiosities into laboratories, the educators who turned them into encyclopaedias, even the buyers of such books were a step above a collector who was aiming at nothing more than social distinction. But there was still something arrogant in the notion that the boundless watery realm of the ocean could be distilled in such a constricted frame as a book or a glass cabinet. As a literal summary of the sea, the cabinet of curiosities was a patent absurdity, but as a symbol it persisted furtively in intellectual history, like a rock that might be exposed when the tide and wind were right.

Later on, water and, eventually, live animals were added to the cabinets. Depending on how much water and which animals, those cabinets were the precursors of the terrarium and the aquarium, a rainforest and an ocean in a box.

When water was poured into the cabinets of curiosities, creating the first aquaria, it seemed to douse the flame of curiosity and undermine the reverence for the unknown; at least the link became attenuated. Most people just collected their lizards or fish, fine sand or interesting-looking rocks, as if the act of collection in itself was satisfying. People spent time appreciating their possessions, live or dead, all these beautiful rarities of form and hue. They had become hobbyists.

In the eighteenth century there was another fad, for filling, or refilling, the cabinets of curiosity with air. But instead of crocodile specimens or fossilised eggs or plants, they kept birds. Parrots, canaries and even 'decorative poultry' were popular, especially among women. People have been wondering about women and their decorative poultry ever since. 'At the height of the Enlightenment,' one historian wrote, 'women were still typically seen as fickle and ill-fated, as helpless creatures of desire, whether for sex or exotic pheasants.' It seems to me a pretty good assessment of the human condition. I guess it went without saying that a girl in the eighteenth century, and for a long time afterwards, might have had a particular reason for identifying with beautiful, brightly coloured creatures in cages.

It's a poignant metaphor, but birds in cages had always looked bored to me. Why would girls do unto the birds as society had done unto them?

'And isn't it a bit cruel,' I asked David, 'to capture marine creatures and put them in a tiny tank in one's home?'

'I keep the tank clean, and don't give them too much work to do. If it's cruel, it's not extremely so.'

But, as I said, David isn't your typical hobbyist. Every weekend he drives to the ocean to get 'fresh' seawater for his fish. He lets the sediment settle and the temperature adjust. Then he puts it in his aquarium cup by cup. He checks the filter and the thermostat, the pH and the oxygenation, to see if everything is working as it should be. Then he examines each and every fish, to see whether they are active or anxious, enervated or ill, easy-going or under attack. There's a little ecosystem in the tank, and he has to keep it in balance. I see the seagrass swaying, and other marine plants, and the different species and colours of fish. I see waves of liquid light flash upon his face.

When he goes to get his weekly bag of ocean water, he goes swimming and diving. From a distance he looks like a fish, rising and sinking in the waves. It's as if he's gone back to a paradise he's always dreamed about, to a home he is still getting to know. Watching him out there, I feel reassured, but also a bit sad.

Of course, he doesn't know how to dance.

David once told me something about himself that I thought was as beautiful as a song.

As a college student he made sure never to take a class on Thursday afternoon. Every Thursday morning, he would get up early, open the curtains and feel the sun with his skin. This was a day for him to spend quality time with himself. It was a day for him to give something back to himself, a day to enjoy.

His classes ended at noon. Whistling to himself, he

walked with relaxed, happy steps out of the gate of the campus, greeting classmates coming the other way. He crossed the street under the underpass, appearing above ground on the other side, and waited for the bus. On the bus, he let the wind that blew in through the window kiss his cheek. The city scenes passed, people got on and off. He knew all the buildings by sight, but everything was new.

He got home, chucked his bookbag on the floor and took off his boots. His elder sister was still at college, his parents were at work, so he was all by himself. He de-capped a bottle of beer and lay down on the sofa and watched an NBA game. When that was done he crouched in front of his aquarium.

He watched the fish swim around, hiding among the plants. The faint vibration of the filter was soothing, the sound of the waves somehow wistful, like a story the universe was telling, sometimes about its origin, sometimes about its fate. He listened, sometimes, to a call that transcended time. Only he could hear it.

He pulled a chair over. He would sit there a bit longer.

When he was finally ready for a brief return to everyday reality, he walked into the kitchen, washed the dishes and put the empty bottle in the bin.

Then he went to his room, got into his bed and started, slowly but surely, to engage in an act that was once called 'self-sullying', but which today is known as 'self-consolation'. He masturbated. It was the highlight of every Thursday afternoon, the final stage of a lengthy ritual. After ejaculating, he took a shower. He might walk over to the basketball court to shoot some hoops. Or he might ride his bike to the baseball field. Sometimes he'd stay in and watch a movie. A bit later his sister would come back from college and his parents from work. When they got home they'd have a family dinner together.

This man was someone with an intuitive understanding that sex was a way of treating yourself well. It was joy, it wasn't the source of pain.

'That's the most romantic thing I've ever heard,' I said, full of admiration and attraction.

But, he said, once he went home on a Thursday, ready for his afternoon ritual, and there was his sister lying on the sofa, laughing her head off at a rerun of some sitcom. All his blissful emotions evaporated. He'd been humming a tune; now he fell silent. The happy time was over before it had begun. He felt angry, resentful. He asked her what she was doing there. The teacher had taken the day off, and there was no class that afternoon. She offered him a crisp.

'No!' he said, sharply.

He started pacing. He went to stand by the aquarium, but he couldn't concentrate. He went to kick around in his room, then came out again.

He found some excuse to be rude to his sister, berating her because she hadn't put the milk back in the fridge.

His sister yelled right back at him. 'What's got into you?'

He spluttered a retort, but ended up saying that it was nothing, sorry, forget it. He paced around some more, then went out.

David would sometimes joke that whenever he had the day off he felt like going out to sea, as a captain or maybe a fisherman. Maybe he wouldn't show up at work the next day. I asked him what I should do, be a fisherman's mate? He said plant flowers. I should plant a garden of my very own.

After I broke my toe, I still accompanied him to the beach every week, but I never joined him in the water. I imagined that if I did it would delay my return to the dance studio. I didn't want to take too much time off.

At the same time I had to admit, as much as I wanted to go back, I also dreaded it. Maybe breaking my toe was a blessing in disguise. It was a way out.

It appeared that I was like the women Donny complained about, women like Susan or Mitsuki. We might start out saying we live for dance, we talk about how dedicated we are to dance, but we don't take it seriously, not really. If we find someone in real life, someone like David, we leave.

Actually, I'd felt frustrated for quite some time. Youlin

had stopped coming. I was tired, and I didn't have much self-esteem left. I felt fragile.

Most importantly, there'd been a subtle change in my friendship with Donny before my accident. I still went to class every week, and often saw him socially. We went out for dinner a lot. But something was different. We still talked and laughed, and discussed dance, but our hearts were no longer so open; we were both holding things in reserve. We were both keeping secrets now. I was and Donny was, too.

But that wasn't the most important thing.

The most important thing was that, after he'd split with Mitsuki and was yet again looking for a new partner, and as a result was on a pretty short fuse, he started losing his temper. 'Your tempo's off in the third bar!' 'Where's the lift in your chest in the fifth bar? Don't slouch!' 'Are you still practising at home?'

Donny yelled at me until I hung my head. And then he kept on yelling.

'Do you ever practise, really practise, what we cover in class? If you don't, it's pointless for you to spend all this time and money, including my time. You might as well just dance in the group class. There you can dance the way you want, do whatever makes you happy.'

In fact, the writing was on the wall. I knew I couldn't keep practising without a partner. I'd made it this far, but

I couldn't make it to the next stage. What was more, I'd reached my physical limit. That was as much as I could do. At least Donny wasn't lying to me. He didn't reassure me that everything would turn out all right if I kept at it.

So maybe I did it on purpose – broke my toe. As it happened, a man had appeared who would take me to the seashore, and who knew how to enjoy himself. Just observing him soothed my anxiety and curiosity, making me feel more rooted, at least for now. I'd been drifting; now I had a home base.

David, someone who had a serious hobby and a steady job, reassured me that ordinary people's lives weren't that scary. He led a simple life. He woke up, went to work, got together with friends, watched his fish and went to the beach at the weekend. He never had any trouble getting to sleep. He was bright and cheerful no matter what.

I still couldn't shake the fear I'd always felt, not completely, of what might happen if I got too close to someone. Although that's exactly what I wanted to do in dance, to pair up with someone, it's unnerving, maybe even unnatural, to get that close. Behind that appealing image of intimacy might be violence and control. I couldn't get over my apprehension, which sometimes turned into desperation.

Perhaps I had too much time on my hands, time that I had been filling up trying to become a dancer. To do that in a different way, I started working, a few editing and proofreading cases at first, then, as my clients introduced me to their friends, more and more. I got busier and busier.

I also spent more and more time with Mitsuki. Actually, I still do. She is as bright-eyed and bushy-tailed as ever. We do yoga together. She got married after she quit dancing and had a kid. She managed to make garden-variety partnership work; maybe, I told myself, I could, too.

A week before my fortieth birthday, a doctor I went to after my periods had stopped announced I had early menopause. The first reaction of every doctor whose second opinion I solicited was surprise, even disbelief, but the battery of tests they all ran confirmed the initial diagnosis. 'It's rare,' they would say, 'but not unheard of.'

One of them said I could take hormones to keep me menstruating. But if I stopped, my periods would stop. It would just be a time for me to adapt, to settle in. It was better not to take them for too long. Hormone therapy over the long term is associated with a higher risk of breast cancer.

I walked out of the hospital, feeling light-headed and shaky. I walked to the side of the road and my legs went soft. I knelt on the sidewalk and started sobbing. This was a rare case of Heaven following human wishes! My wish had finally been granted. I remembered my despair at about age fourteen when I'd heard someone say that daughters would grow up to be just like their mothers. I was distraught; it was too much to take. I started hating Heaven, because the pain, the anguish, the aimlessness of life that I saw epitomised in her would keep getting passed down for ever. At the time I was still too young to be able to express myself in these terms, but what I lacked in eloquence I made up for in courage. I cursed Heaven, vowing that I would never have children of my own. Heaven heard my curse as a plea, and Heaven eventually relented: it would end with me.

How had she put it, the old female technician who read my ultrasound and X-ray? 'Your uterus is shrunken,' she had said. Then she showed me. I saw my uterus among all the other organs, which looked humungous in contrast. It was as if it was hiding shyly, trying not to be seen. It was a microcosm of me.

Meixin would often message me at the weekend, asking what I was up to.

I'd answer by asking her the same thing.

She always said she was debugging programs on her computer or apps on her mobile.

One time I asked if her fiancé – the new one – was there. Why didn't she go to a movie, go on a date? Why was she at home?

'He's gone shopping with my mother.'

Another time, not long after that, she nudged me in the middle of the night, saying she didn't know where to find Prince Charming, where she could meet a suitable boy. She felt stifled.

'Your fiancé?'

'We're still together, but he's unsuitable. My mum says he's got problems.'

'Him too?' At least it hadn't gone on as long as the previous one.

'Long story.'

'Break the engagement? Let each other go?'

'No. I can't tell you all the details, but I suggested separating, and he got really angry. He said me and my mother are insufferable. It shouldn't have to be this complicated.'

Part of me kept the faith that one day I would go back to dance, because Donny was still competing and teaching. However long he competed for, I thought he would go on teaching his whole life. If I sought him out, I could return to the world of dancing. That's all I had to do. We were so good together; we had been so close.

But then, when I started freelancing as an editor-proofreader, a couple of years went by and I hesitated. Three more years passed.

I heard Donny had quit his job at the pharmaceutical company and started teaching for a living. I was surprised.

He'd gone and done what he despised the most. He was selling his body for money, so to speak. He had tied his love to his livelihood. Now that he was teaching for a living, he had classes all day long – sometimes in his teacher's studio, sometimes in the gym. He took on group classes. He even took the train down as far south as Hsinchu, an hour each way, to teach them. Had he changed? I heard that he had a new partner and was dancing really well.

He still wanted to go to Blackpool, and this might be his last chance. No wonder he was giving it his all.

I called him a few times after that, telling him I wanted to take classes again.

'Problem is I still don't have a partner. Now that you've got even more students, can you look out for me?'

'All right, but you know how hard it is. Why don't you ask your friends? If you find someone, bring them along to the group class. Or come and look around for yourself, see if there's anyone who can lead you when his partner's resting.'

I knew what he'd left unsaid: my age and condition. I knew that as well as anyone. But what surprised me was his tone. He'd started to give me the standard line, and with a hint of officialese. It was the spiel dance teachers usually spout to students who are clingy or demanding.

A while later I called him again, and asked if he'd looked out for me.

I heard a sharp intake of breath. 'You know it's a long shot,' he said.

'Then I'll take a class with you at the studio. You can lead me just like you used to!'

'Sorry, I don't have the time. My timetable is full.'

'Not even an hour a week? Can you please see if you can fit me in?'

'All right, I'll let you know.'

After that he stopped taking my calls.

I tried every so often, but he never answered.

I felt really low. Had he become like all those teachers I'd had before I'd discovered him, the teachers who only had eyes for competitors or rich ladies, now that he was doing it for a living? Had he really become a talent snob? Was he doing it for the money now, not for students like me, who didn't have a fortune or a competitive future?

I always knew I'd never be his equal in dance, or be able to fatten his wallet. But didn't he need any sincere, honest friends? I could at least give him that. Perhaps he'd never needed or wanted it, and our friendship had never been as mutual as I had assumed.

Finally, I'd had enough. It was too cruel of him to cut me off like that. He didn't want me as a friend, as a student, or even as a cash cow. He didn't want me in any way.

*

I'd had enough. Now I would really put it behind me, I thought. But then I was often reminded that I had dancing in my blood, and in my bones. My feet would often start moving on their own, doing the rumba steps. Then I would miss the strenuous days I'd spent shuttling to and from the studio and the activity centre. I looked back fondly on all the hard work I'd done. Of course I would, in a cascade of memories and emotions, think about Donny. I wondered where he'd made it to. Did he still want to go to Blackpool? It had been such a long time – maybe he was too old now, like me. I checked his Facebook, but didn't see any updates. I asked Meixin, but she knew as much as I did. She asked Mrs Lai.

Donny had passed away, less than a week before.

Mrs Lai said he'd been losing weight, until he was looking quite gaunt. He was complaining of nausea, too. He thought it was a cold of some kind, maybe flu, but he just couldn't shake it. He took a day off to go to the hospital for tests, and that day off turned into the rest of his life, such as it was. He had lymphoma. There was nothing they could offer him except palliative care. Three weeks later he was gone.

It was raining the day of Donny's memorial service. I went with Meixin. It was held at one of the local universities, in an auditorium, but it was still packed. Class after class, team after team, all his students had come to pay their respects. I didn't get anywhere near his spirit tablet, nor did I bow and burn incense in front of his blown-up image. I didn't pay my respects to his parents, either. I just looked at his pictures and watched his videos, an AV album of his dance career.

Quite a few students had cried their eyes out. They must have seen the good in Donny, too. I imagined that Donny was there in the auditorium somewhere or somehow. To see everyone gathered there must be no small consolation to him as a teacher. But as a dancer? What was he feeling now, about all his striving? Had he been able to shine? Had he made it into his secret world?

Afterwards, I walked with Meixin through the rain into the MRT station. We sat next to each other on the train. Only then did I see the marks that time had left on her face. It wasn't wrinkles; her skin wasn't sagging – not at all, not yet. It was exhaustion. Her lips were dry and she had a pallor; she was haggard. She had a dazed expression, as if her spirit had been summoned into some realm of torment. I was struck by how many years had passed, by how old we were. We were middle-aged women now, but she looked exactly the same as she had in the studio the first time I saw her a decade before. She had the same straight long hair, a fringe to her eyebrows. She wore the same navy pea coat with two rows of buttons, the same white blouse, the same Mary Janes. This must have been the appearance her mother thought a young lady ought to have. She had the look of an ingénue in a Japanese TV drama. She'd had this look from fourteen years old to forty.

Her mother wanted her daughter to be a girl for ever, never to marry, never to grow up. Meixin could keep working and supporting the family and her mother would always be the most important person in her life. That way the mother would never get old.

Maybe I was being melodramatic.

'You know you're not supposed to go home right after a funeral,' I said. 'You have to go somewhere with a lot of people and walk around, have a coffee, go to a department store. I've got an appointment in a bit, but Sogo's on the way. Do you want to come shopping with me?'

She smiled. Her eyes were still like crescent moons. 'Sure,' she said. 'But I can't buy anything myself.'

'Why not?'

'I might buy the wrong thing.'

'What's wrong with buying the wrong thing? If you regret it, exchange it. At any event, it's your money, you can spend it how you want.'

'You're right,' she acquiesced. But then she squinted, as if trying to smile. 'But I'd better not, I should go home.'

I looked at her in disbelief.

'I do go shopping, I really do. But not on my own. I don't have taste. My mother didn't pass hers down to me, she

kept it to herself. The clothes I choose don't flatter me, so she chooses everything for me. It's for my own good ... '
She was going on and on. She looked over at me. 'What mother wouldn't try to do the best for her children?'

I smiled at her, then slowly nodded, giving her the answer she wanted. Then I went back to watching our reflections in the window.

At some level, she must know she's pretending. What else would explain her haggard appearance? Why else would she have said that?

She posts pictures of herself on Facebook working out or meeting new friends. Lately, she mentioned her mother has helped her arrange a meeting with 'a nice young man'. She asked her friends to help her choose the most beautiful photo to send him. On Mother's Day she posted a photo of herself with her mother, gushing in the message about how grateful she was for everything. Meixin smiled her usual smile, consistently cute. Her mother's face was pixelated.

10

LONELY GHOSTS

I dreamed my father arranged to meet me in a café, just the two of us. He was trying to tell me something. I could see his lips moving, and I could hear his voice, but it was as if we were underwater, and his words too distorted for me to comprehend.

When I woke up the dream seemed like a parable, not just about my father and me, but about my mother, too. We once had the status of a family, and lived as a social unit, but I felt like an orphan. So did my parents. We each lived bravely, rudely, roughly. We kept our feelings bottled up inside, and though my mother let off a lot of steam it wasn't enough. We never managed to connect with each other, or feel for each other in our isolation. Success came naturally to us, along with security. But never intimacy.

Loneliness ran in the family. Each lonely person left

another lonely, and the other's loneliness caused yet another to be lonely, but without allowing anyone to understand. At times we felt an attraction, and tried to come together, but when we met the magnets turned the other way and pushed us apart.

We lived like each other's lonely ghosts.

But maybe that wasn't quite it, or all there was to it. I guessed that what my father had been trying to tell me in the café was part of the story of his childhood. He did that from time to time. It would come out of nowhere.

He grew up in Keelung, an old port city to the northeast of Taipei. When he was about five or six years old, his father – my paternal grandfather – took him on a boat back to Foochow in China, hoping there would be more work there than there was in Keelung. If there wasn't, they could at least stay with relatives.

Grandfather was a traditional carpenter, a joiner. He'd learned a craft that's mostly been lost, where the artisan makes a piece of furniture without a single nail.

They didn't buy a proper ticket, just went to a pier where you could pay a bit of money to get on a boat that was going to cross the Taiwan Strait.

Unbeknown to them, a massacre broke out in Keelung the next day – on 8 March 1947. Men were forced to kneel on either side of the canal that runs through the city to the piers, shot from behind and pushed in, until the water was red with blood. Nobody dared to go out and check for missing family members, let alone collect the bodies, not until the fourth or fifth day. By then the corpses were putrid.

At the time, my parents were both children. They were living in the same city but hadn't met yet. My maternal grandmother was too sad to cry when she realised her eldest son, one of my uncles, was not coming back, though he did just that several days later. When they were arresting people, he'd ducked into the stairwell of some building and listened to the sound of killing outside. When he made it home, his mother pushed him frantically upstairs, telling him to get into bed. She wrapped him up in a heavy blanket, went downstairs and locked the front door. She went into the back garden, picked enough vegetables to last them a few days, piled them in the kitchen, locked the back door and ordered all the kids to stay put.

A hundred and fifty miles west-northwest, my father and his father got off the boat and took a bus from the harbour into the city, only to find Foochow razed. It had been a battlefield, but now the civil war between the Communists and the Nationalists had moved on. My grandfather asked around, but of course there was no work. Everyone he met was destitute. Nobody had the means to have a piece of custom furniture made. They took another bus to the village where his relatives were living last he heard, but they were all dead, or had fled or gone mad. My young father was starving, but not scared. My grandfather squeezed his hand and managed a moment of self-deprecation. He'd taken his wife across the sea to Keelung to try to make a living, and had returned with his son to Foochow for the same reason. They'd gone desperately hungry with shrivelled-up stomachs on both sides of the Taiwan Strait.

Father and son held out there a month, until there was truly nothing left. They had no choice but to try to get back to Keelung. Nobody said anything on the boat, because nobody knew what had happened.

When they went ashore they noticed that even the colour of the sky was harsh – a dead grey. Half the city had died. Worry and sorrow enveloped the place like fog. Only then did my father and grandfather hear what had happened in the month they were gone.

It was not until a few days later that the horror sank in. It was as if they'd been swept into a fold in time, a fortuitous one as it turned out, only to be flung out again.

It was fate, my father said.

My grandfather was not my father's birth father. My father was the youngest of nine siblings. After the war in the Pacific had started to go against the Japanese, the Taiwanese people had it rough. It was a time of great privation, especially for my father's family. His parents had both died – first his father, then his mother. Father was still in swaddling clothes. There was no way his siblings could take care of him, so they basically gave him away. His eldest brother and sister sold him to that joiner and his wife for a bit of money. Later on, his brothers and sisters and the joiner and his wife moved separately to Keelung. They lived across the harbour from one another, at opposite ends of the city. Each heard that the other was there, but they never got in touch.

My father only found out his siblings were living on the other side of the city when he was in his fifties. He got in touch immediately. Although he had always been cold to everyone in his life, he was all worked up about it, because he was going to seek his roots. He was a hard man, he didn't cry, but he was as excited as any little boy would have been. He dressed up and went to meet the eldest sister, the one who'd made the decision to sell him, along with his fourth-eldest brother. They didn't hug; they just shook hands, smiling. They tried to get to know each other, asked what they had done in life and what they were doing now. The grandkids were running around in the family room.

A sense of separation, an acknowledgement of unfamiliarity, grew in my dad's excitement. It was natural, he felt. He hadn't seen them in over fifty years, and had no memory of them.

Several days later, his eldest sister got their fourth brother to come over for a visit. She said they'd talked it over several times and decided to tell him. They wanted him to know the truth. The truth was that he was only a half-brother; he never would have shared a surname with them. Their father had died, and they'd had to move, over and over again. Their mother took up with a man in one of the places they had moved to. That man had lived with them for a while, but then he left, leaving the mother pregnant. My father was an accident.

That was why he was so much younger than the others. That was also why, after their mother had died, they were able to sell him, an infant in swaddling clothes, to a total stranger, without a second thought.

In ethology, biological distance is defined as the closest distance at which two organisms of the same species can get along. Any closer and they'll feel discomfort, or intense irritation, as if their space has been invaded. The only options then are flight or fight.

Some animals have a bigger biological distance, some smaller.

Ballroom dancing clearly contravenes the norm of biological distance for human beings.

Two people, who might be spouses, lovers, strangers or enemies, have to rub intimately against each other, touching parts of each other's bodies that normally nobody would be allowed to touch. It is fundamentally invasive to stay in such close quarters for too long.

No matter how satisfying such physical contact might be, it compromises a person's most basic biological sense of security.

At the happiest time in my studies with Donny, the time when we were the closest, I was excited about going to every class, and every class was hot and spicy. But there was one time, after class, when I'd changed clothes and walked out of the studio, that I realised I was shaking. I felt as if I had been assaulted, in a sexual sense.

I had no idea where the feeling came from. One minute I was fine, the next minute I was swept up in a tidal wave of fury. I lost it. I ran out of the studio, ran to my car, slammed the door and slammed my fists on the steering wheel. I screamed at the top of my lungs. Then I sat there, dazed.

It was the longest time before I could calm down. What had just happened? The class had gone the same as usual: dancing, practice, correction, more practice. It had gone really well, actually. I'd danced well, and Donny had been in a good mood. It hadn't hurt that the weather had been fine. It was a sunny day.

Then I smelled it – a mixture of Donny's cologne, his sweat and my sweat. We'd been doing the rumba, embracing each other again and again. Every time we pressed together the fluids that covered our bodies and the vapours that enveloped them mixed together and penetrated my open follicles.

My head and heart told me one thing, that dance was happiness and excitement. But my body gave me another kind of message: it was invasive.

Last year I called Mrs Lai and asked about the aunties and uncles. How was everyone? She said they were still dancing, but with far fewer people. The new teacher had a very different style. A lot of students had stopped coming, or stopped coming as often, because they couldn't get used to it. Of course, some of them had had to ease off for health reasons.

'You want to come to a class?' she asked.

It took me a while to find the new venue. It was in a different building, a new activity centre. They'd moved to make it more convenient for the new teacher.

He had a terrible temper. When an auntie or uncle kept asking questions about some sequence, he would lose his patience. Exasperated, he would give dancers who were old enough to be his parents a piece of his mind.

'Didn't I just tell you? How many times do I have to explain it?'

I thought of Donny, who would explain clearly and methodically no matter who asked or how many times they asked, until the student understood. Donny never lost his patience or his temper. Certainly not with the aunties and uncles. He would answer one student's question, then wait for the next. He would keep answering questions during break.

Fat chance of asking this teacher a question during break. He would pretend he hadn't heard.

Of course, he was teaching individual classes. He preferred the students in the group class to take an individual class because, he claimed, he could explain things more clearly. But he still sounded impatient, and somehow supercilious, giving me this spiel, as if I wasn't worth his time.

I asked Mrs Lai how she thought he compared to Donny.

She laughed and said they'd just keep dancing. 'Who knows if we'll still be dancing a year from now?' She and Mr Lai were in their seventies now. They weren't too demanding.

Though it was a lot of money – no freebies or even discounts, just because I happened to be Donny's student – I signed up for a month's worth of individual classes with the new teacher, just to see. If he'd been irritating in the group class, he was insufferable one on one. If he hadn't explained something clearly, or if for whatever reason I hadn't understood, he got snippy. Why am I paying you to yell at me? I wondered.

As a dancer, he was also quite a contrast with Donny. He mainly danced standard ballroom: the waltz, the tango and other slow, elegant dances. The rich ladies he spent most of his time on liked the waltz because of their level of physical fitness and the nature of the dance. It didn't require a lot of energy or strength, so they could dance for a long time, until they were old. This teacher taught Latin when he had to, but his heart obviously wasn't in it. His dancing felt forced, and his choreography lacked creativity. He, too, lacked the necessary physical fitness.

On one occasion, at a student performance he'd organised at a dance hall, he asked me if I wanted to learn the waltz instead. It was a suggestion, not a question.

He danced a lot of dances at the performance, with his rich lady students. They'd spent a fortune on the decorations, and the main sponsor, the richest of all the rich ladies, changed costumes twice.

After it was over, I overheard him chatting with a few of the uncles from our group class. They were teasing the teacher, asking him how it felt dancing with all those rich ladies day after day, year in, year out.

'Like holding an ATM,' he said. He only had to do it for another ten years and he would never have to worry about money again. It was supposed to be a joke, but he didn't sound too proud of himself when he told it.

You're not such a pleasure to hold yourself, I thought. He

actually smelled – of polyester and sweat. Donny sweated, too, of course – he was only human – but he always packed a few extra clean T-shirts in his backpack, in case his body odour bothered his student or his partner.

Donny wasn't just a good dancer and teacher, he was also a considerate human being. The new teacher was none of the above.

He still owed me a few classes, but I wasn't ever going to take them. I never wanted to see him again. I wasn't going to let him sully my memory of my time in the halls of dance.

I will never dance again, I thought, walking home that night. But I wasn't angry, or sad, or lost at the thought that all my struggles were over. I wasn't disappointed at having been left out in the cold, excluded from the world of partner dance, which was how I'd always felt during my scrappy days as Donny's student. It wasn't as if I'd let myself down. It wasn't as if I'd let anyone else down, either, especially Donny.

Here I am, Donny, I said. Look where I've ended up, look how far I've come.

Once I swam in the shimmering light of the sun; here I am, in the moonlight, but I can see more clearly now.

I used to wear 2½-inch heels; now I wear flat-soled shoes.

I failed to become a dancer, but I did become a woman.

Donny, it seems, heard me. He answered with a memory.

I always arrived early for the individual class, and practised my basic rumba steps, doing the rounds of the studio classroom over and over again. Sometimes I got tired, and Donny would appear and tell me not to give up. When I got so tired I couldn't maintain the pace, he would clap for me, slower and slower so I could keep up. At other times, he would appear by my side and silently do the rounds with me.

When we were finally done, I'd collapse on the floor, out of breath. He would help me up.

There was one time I had a tantrum. 'I hate doing the rumba steps, it's tiring and boring!' I whined.

When he laughed out loud, I went into a litany. 'You have to count your steps while rocking your hips, you have to glide, you have to stay erect, and then you have to do all these things while following the music. It's so hard!'

'You're wrong there, Summer. You're overanalysing. You're making dance a lot more complicated than it needs to be. You're trying to dance rumba with your brain. No wonder you find it hard. It's just walking down the street, girl, that's it. You have to forget the idea of dancing. All dancing is walking down the street, in this really smooth, fluid, elaborate way, walking with your head held high.

'That's all we really need in our lives, Summer, to walk beautifully. That's all there is.'